GW00391729

'There was only one thing to worry about in the whole world . . . and that was not to die.'

Against a background of plans for a fashionable new yachting marina, transforming the quiet Essex fishing-village of Birdsmarsh, Paul and his friend Gus aboard their fishing smack *Swannie* become involved in events that nearly cost Paul his life.

"There was only one thing to worry about in the whole world . . . and that was not to die."

Against a background of plans for a fashionable new yachting marina transforming the quiet Essex fishing village of Birdsmarsh, Paul and his friend Gus aboard their fishing smack Swanna become involved in events that nearly cost Paul his life.

'*He's* keen! You cunning ass! I bet it was your idea before it was Sydney's.'

'All right,' Gus admitted. 'But Sydney's dying to help. "By Jove, boy, splendid plan!" and all that.' By tucking his under jaw under his top lip, Gus gave a very fair imitation of Sydney Peacemaker, the president of the East Coast Smack Preservation Society, who kept his own smack, *Phoebe*, in the local harbour.

Paul sighed again. He wasn't a fighter by nature, and could see that his 'den' was to be wrested from him, cleared of its homely conglomeration of half-finished carvings, birds' eggs, driftwood, broken guitar, pop cans, camera, notebooks and similar impedimenta, and put to sea all scrubbed and shipshape. He knew he ought to be keen to see it happen, like Gus; the sea ought to be in his blood. His father might be a farmer, but at least he was a farmer whose farm boasted two miles of sea-wall. That meant that he positively owned a good deal of sea when the tide was up, which was more than Gus's father could boast. Paul's uncle, owner of *Swansong* until his death five years ago, had been a fisherman, and so had his mother's father. But it made no difference. Paul had never wanted to sail.

'I don't see that it will make any difference to you,' Gus said. 'After all, you can still use her same as you do now—keep her a bit tidier, though. And she'll rot to bits if she's left neglected much longer, then she won't be of any use to anyone. She's in a pretty awful state.'

'Yes.' Paul could only agree. Then he remembered something else. 'She's supposed to be an unlucky boat. What about that? Do you remember what they all said when my uncle died?'

'Why, do you believe all that rot?'

'No, but a lot of people who know better do. Your father, for instance.'

'He's one of the old school,' Gus said with a slight bitterness. 'She's never been unlucky for you,' he pointed out.

'She's not had the chance, sitting here,' Paul said.

'She's not had the chance to be anything.' Gus pounced eagerly.

Paul felt irritated, but did not want to argue any more. He pushed the bones into a defeated heap on the table, put the top on the glue and went up on deck. Gus started fiddling with the engine, and Paul stood hunched, his hands in his pockets, staring at the water. He was an angular boy, heron-like in his grey polo-necked jersey and narrow, muddy jeans. He had yellowish, untidy hair lapping at the edge of his jersey neck, a pale, bony face and short-sighted grey eyes. For a bird-lover, his eyesight was hopeless. He had to wear glasses for work, and his binoculars were his most precious possession. When it had been discovered that he was short-sighted, when he was ten, he could still remember his amazement on first wearing glasses and finding out what he had been missing all that time. One of the few times he had ever been out in a boat, with Gus's father, Gus had been reading the names on buoys when Paul had scarcely been able to distinguish the buoy itself, a fact which he now, obtusely, held against sailing.

The tide was sliding up over the saltings, sluggish on this still, February day. Behind him, over the sea-wall, was his father's farm—it would be his when he left school and got down to work on it, and no thought pleased him more—and at his feet was the North Sea pushing its way up the Blackwater valley, its grey breast uncommonly peaceful on this dull winter Saturday. Paul was to remember the day all his life, yet at that moment, as he stood regarding the sea, there was nothing remarkable in the landscape, nor in his mind. He saw Mersea, a mound of grey trees against the low cloud, two miles across the water; some gulls crying out by the Nass beacon and, way out in the limits of his visibility, a grey blob which he knew to be a gravel barge making up the Colne. From where *Swannie* lay in a cradle of mud and grass that flooded at high water, the shore changed direction, bending away southward and leaving the river to the mercies of the open sea. If he looked to the east, there was nothing but sea between him and Holland. His father's cows grazed to the sea-wall, and the tide rubbed unceasingly at the narrow strip of shingle beach where the sandpipers flittered and driftwood with foreign lettering lay scattered for *Swannie*'s stove. Paul knew it as intimately as anyone alive; it was his territory. His short-sighted eyes had seen more along the sea-wall and shore in fifteen years than his father's had seen in fifty. He had no wish to be anywhere else or to do any-

thing else other than what he did. He had no ambition; he only wanted the farm, and life to go on as it always had, and that was why Gus had the power to irritate, with his plans and improvements Gus. was a restless person. He knew what he wanted, too, but, unlike Paul, he was frustrated in his ambitions. He had a tyrannical father who fished for a living and got drunk most of the rest of the time. Paul supposed he should help Gus, but Gus, for all his frustrations, seemed perfectly able to look after himself. He was tough and capable and clever. Paul was sure that, in the end, he would get what he wanted, as he always had up till now, even *Swannie* sailing.

Gus whistled cheerfully from below deck as he primed the ancient petrol-paraffin engine. He knew Paul was put out, and was thinking round for something to say.

'Who does your father know with a white Jag?' he shouted

up. 'There was one turning in your drive when I came past. London registration. Nobody I've ever seen before.'

'Traveller, I expect,' Paul said.

'What, in a Jag?' Gus sounded sceptical. 'Very glossy job for a traveller. Besides, he was too fat and well-dressed. Towny type.'

'Someone to say we've come up on our Premium Bond,' Paul suggested hopefully.

He had gone below again and was looking round *Swannie*'s small cabin critically, wondering what it would be like in motion, heeling and bouncing to a fresh breeze. It was very small, being just the area before the mast. The rusty coal-stove, and the two bunks with a table between them, filled it completely. A steep companion-way led up to the forehatch, and beside the mast a low opening hacked in the bulkhead gave access to what had once been the fish-hold. It was lit by a glass panel let into the main hatch and was much bigger than the cuddy forward, but the boys preferred the cuddy in the winter because it had the stove in it. They wanted to build a raised cabin-top over the main hatch and convert the hold into a proper saloon, but they had never seemed to get the job started. Paul wasn't very handy at carpentry, and Gus preferred to spend his time on the engine. But now, Paul thought, it looked as if *Swannie* was going to get her refit. If Sydney was interested, there was no knowing how she would end up.

He looked at her thoughtfully, leaning, stooped, against the hefty, smooth bulk of her mast. It was right that she should sail, only he did not want her taken over, out of his hands. He would have to learn the sailing business, too, and use the right words, and know how it all worked, and he knew it wouldn't come easily to him. Like putting the bird together. He was a fumbler and a bungler and a dreamer; he was always being told so. He was no good at school, for ever being compared unfavourably with his brilliant brother Chris, no good with practical things, only with cows and birds and music and 'suchlike women's things', as Gus teased him. 'A right yokel', Gus called him, but Paul took no offence. Only now, if *Swannie* had to sail, he didn't want to be an ass.

'Stand back!' Gus grinned, and flung himself on the fly-wheel.

Some choking explosions echoed through the hold, and then a monstrous rattling seized the old smack, so that she quivered from stem to stern. Paul grimaced, and Gus obligingly throttled the noise down, so that the rattling changed to a not unpleasant thumping.

'There, how's that? She's not forgotten how, has she?' Gus came back through the hold, looking pleased with himself. 'Do her the world of good to run for a bit.'

'I thought she was supposed to be a sailing-boat?'

'Yes, but that's no reason for letting a perfectly good engine go to pot. Your uncle put it in. It's not bad, considering its age.'

Paul looked at Gus curiously. 'I can't think why you're so mad at your father's making you an apprentice at Mason's, when you like engines. The way you were talking about it, anyone would think you were going to work in purgatory. If you hate the idea, why do you like fiddling with *Swannie*'s old works so much?'

He felt an obtuse desire to needle Gus, because Gus was in one of his 'taking-over' moods. But as soon as he saw Gus's expression darken he felt mean.

'Because this engine is a boat engine, dim-wit. Mason's is a filthy old tip for broken-down lorries. No one in his senses could possibly want to spend his life working in a place like that.'

'Is it fixed up, then? Doesn't your father know how you feel about it?'

'Of course he does, but he doesn't care whether I'll like it or not. He reckons a mechanic is a good steady job. With prospects, he says. Prospects of rotting away with boredom, I told him, but he just laughed. I'm to start in July, as soon as I leave school.'

Gus had forgotten his prowess with *Swannie*'s engine, and had flung himself down on the bunk. He glowered at Paul's bird bones. 'There's only one thing I'm interested in, and he knows it. And just because he's too lazy to make a decent living at it he doesn't think anyone else can. He says fishing is finished.' Paul, who was familiar with the sight of *Emma*, Gus's father's old smack, chuntering about the estuary with her trawl out, was not surprised at this opinion.

'Well, his sort is, perhaps. There's not many new smacks

around, are there? No young blokes going in for it, that I know of. Fishing is big business now, not a family thing round the shore like it used to be.'

'I know all that,' Gus said impatiently. 'But boats aren't finished, are they? There's not only fishing, if you've got a decent boat. You can take charter parties out in the summer; and fish in the winter. I wouldn't mind anything with boats, even working my time as a carpenter in one of the yards at Burnham—why, even being dog's-body in a chandler's or something. But he just won't have it.'

'I suppose he might if there was something handy here. A boat-yard or something.'

'There's nothing here, that's the trouble,' Gus said.

'No.' If Paul hadn't got the farm, he knew he'd have to go away to work, too. They all did, when they left school. The nearest town, and that was small enough, was fourteen miles away. Their small village, once a busy little port with a fleet of barges plying in and out to take away the hay and grain produced in the neighbourhood, was now the forgotten dead end of a peninsula framed by tidal water. Paul would not have had it any different for a fortune, but he was perfectly familiar with the local complaint. Apart from farming, there was no work. He wished he hadn't said anything. Gus's face had gone miserable at the contemplation of his fate, closed up and mutinous. He could be as stubborn and violent as his father if he felt like it, Paul knew. In looks he took after him too; he was stocky and agile, like the fisherman, with thick dark hair and scornful brown eyes. Like his father, he got into trouble easily, but, unlike his father, he was clever and cheerful and resilient. Only the thought of being a garage mechanic had the power to depress him for long.

'Learning engines is a good trade, anyway,' Paul said. 'You'll be able to turn it to boats when you're old enough to please yourself.'

'Yes, that's what I tell myself,' Gus said. 'And if I save hard enough I'll have a boat of some sort in time.'

'There's always *Swannie*,' Paul said, ashamed of himself for checking Gus's ebullience so successfully, and now anxious to make amends.

'Yeah, if we can somehow get our hands on the gear to fit her out.' Gus brightened visibly. 'I dare say my father's got some stuff that'll do for rigging—good enough for a bit. It's just if Sydney can find us some sails.'

'If he's a proper preservationist, he's bound to, isn't he?' Paul said. 'Isn't it their life's work, keeping the old smacks in commission?'

This made them both laugh. Sydney was a doctor from London who made the local harbour his spare-time base. His society was considered a great lark by the local population, who thought it would be more use if it were converted to the East Coast Smacks*men's* Preservation Society. But it had its uses as it was, for when some broken-down smack had seen its day it usually found a buyer in a city-based friend of Sydney's with the same romantic notions of restoring the old craft to all its pristine glory.

'You going to wait here for Sydney, then?' Paul said. He started to gather the bones of the diver together in a tea-towel. 'I'd better get back for dinner. I might come down again after milking.'

'Mmm. I'll wait for him.'

Gus went back aft to the engine, and Paul went up on deck. The tide had turned, and he threw the bones out on to the water, where they swirled round in a small eddy, then slipped away between the mud banks.

He put his gum boots on and jumped over on to the saltings. The beaten track up on to the sea-wall was a glistening quagmire, laced with stranded seaweed, but the sea-wall and the fields beyond were hard and dried out from the February winds. Birdsmarsh, his home farm which took its name from the village, lay to seaward of the village, a huddle of old buildings in the middle of reclaimed pasture. A scrub of elm protected it from the east; otherwise it was a bleak spot. From *Swannie* it was a half-mile walk; to the nearest road it was a half-mile to the west, down a straight drive bordered with the survivors of an avenue of elms. Paul hurried across the fields, watching the plovers wheeling up against the grey sky. People always said of Birdsmarsh, 'Well, it's all right in summer . . .' Paul laughed at their hesitancy. Poor Chris's first and short-lived girl friend, down for Christmas with him from Cambridge, had spent the entire holiday expressing amazement at their splendid isolation, and on her return had given Chris up in preference for a youth from Surbiton. 'She was a fool,' Paul thought, remembering. The farm-house faced him as he came through the last gate, whitewashed and four-square, with small windows and sagging tiled roof. It had managed to stand up there for two hundred years; the Dutch barn beside it, built a mere ten years ago, looked brash by comparison. The cowsheds were half old, half new, straggling round two muddy yards. Set incongruously before them, the white Jaguar that Gus had mentioned made Paul lift his eyebrows in surprise.

'Dad was going out at ten,' he remembered. But his father's Land-Rover was still in the barn. 'He must be important, whoever he is.'

Curious, he pushed open the kitchen door and went indoors, shaking his boots off in the porch. The big room was warm and steamy with cooking, but the table was not laid, nor was his mother in evidence. But from his father's study next door Paul could hear the sound of voices, his mother's included. The visitor's voice was unfamiliar. Paul let the back door slam, as evidence that he was home, and went and stood by the Aga. He heard the door open in the study and his mother called, 'Paul, is that you?'

'Yes, Mum.'

She said something about the dinner to the visitor, and came across the hall into the kitchen. She went to the oven and opened it, looking at its contents in an abstracted manner. Paul's curiosity grew stronger.

'Who is it?' he asked. 'Is something up?'

'Not exactly,' his mother said. But there was something in her manner quite strange to Paul. She looked worried, and half-excited, and completely absorbed by whatever it was the visitor had been talking about. The pie in the oven was burnt, which normally would have had her tut-tutting with dismay, but now she scarcely seemed to notice it. She put it on the table and said, 'There you are. Put it back when you've had what you want.'

'Why, aren't you having any?'

'Later. When Mr.—er, this man has finished.' She looked at Paul in a searching way, which made him anxious.

'What is it? Who is he?' Paul asked.

'Oh, Paul,' his mother said. She opened her mouth to say something more, then obviously thought better of it. Her expression was one of compassion. She was looking at him, he thought, as if he had grown another head.

'Whatever's the matter?'

But she shook her head suddenly, and said, 'Oh, nothing, perhaps. We'll be finished in a minute. Take what you want. There are some baked apples in there for afters.'

She went back to the study, taking the oven-cloth with her. Paul had never seen her so preoccupied.

'Perhaps it is our Premium Bond,' he thought, cutting a large portion out of the pie. But she hadn't looked exactly happy. Paul felt a nasty twinge of doubt. His mother wasn't given to displays of emotion. She was a down-to-earth, dependable, good-natured woman. Why the 'Oh, Paul'? he wondered. He ate hungrily, but didn't really notice what it was he was eating.

2
THE VISITOR'S PLAN

Gus decided to go down to the harbour to see if Sydney was there. Now that Paul had digested the idea of *Swansong*'s sailing again, Gus was keen to get on with it. His father wouldn't let him sail *Emma*, but he wouldn't be able to stop him from sailing *Swannie*. It was only Sydney's saying he might be able to find the sails for her that had set Gus seriously thinking about getting the boat moving. Sail-less, it had never been feasible. He hoped desperately that Sydney meant what he had said, that it wasn't just an offhand encouragement. People who had plenty of money, as Sydney seemed to have, could be singularly dim, Gus often thought, towards beggars like himself. 'If you want to sail, whatever's to stop you, living in a place like this?' Sydney and his friends would say, as if living in the place automatically laid on the boat and its gear, all in running order. Boats—of a kind—there were in plenty. The harbour was full of run-down work boats and leaking dinghies. But of boats a man would trust himself to go to sea in there were exactly two: Sydney Peacemaker's *Phoebe* and the yacht *Woodwind*.

Birdsmarsh harbour—if such it could be called—was a slit of mud protected from the estuary by a long, narrow island running parallel to the shore. At high water one could sail in one side and out (if one was careful) at the other. The island would then be just about covered. At low water the channel was meagre, trickling to a standstill some yards from the quay. A deep-keel boat like *Woodwind* could just lie afloat in one of the deep holes. The island then stood up bare, a desolate lump of isolated salting with whale-like flanks of shining mud. Looking at the scene from the sea-wall, Gus well understood that it could hardly be called a yachtsman's paradise. Only to mud-conditioned yachtsmen, at least. Or cranks like Sydney who got lyrical about the peace and quiet. The 'damn-all, desperate nothingness', as Gus described it. It was all right for Sydney, getting away from it all. He was lucky he had something to get away from. Gus often wished he had.

'It's not that you're a bad place,' he thought, his eyes on the ebbing mud as he walked along the sea-wall towards the quay, 'not if you had something to offer.' That was what he had against Birdsmarsh. This feeling was creeping up on Gus like a flooding tide, because he was to leave school in July. He didn't particularly want to leave, but his father wouldn't let him stay on another year, as Paul was going to. 'Waste of flaming time,' his father said. Gus pushed his hands sullenly into his pockets. Below him *Emma* lay heeled on the mud. Beyond her, Sydney's *Phoebe* lay to her anchor, as shining and smart as *Emma* was unkempt.

Sydney was coming along the sea-wall towards him. He hadn't forgotten, after all, which Gus hoped was a good sign. His large, ungainly figure was unmistakable. His face shone with good nature. He was about sixty, yet he had a gauche, boyish manner, and a touching eagerness, that did not go with his age.

'Hullo, there!' he shouted at Gus. 'I was just coming along to see you. You going off now?'

'No. I was coming to see if you were around, as a matter of fact.'

'Excellent.' Sydney beamed. He came to a halt in front of Gus, planting his enormous gum boots squarely. He wore his usual unyachty tweed suit with the baggy, darned trousers and a fair-isle pullover with ladders all up the front of it. An oilskin was slung on his shoulder. He paused as Gus turned round to go back the way he had come, and nodded down to *Emma*.

'That your father's smack?' he said.

'Yes.' Gus stopped to look at her too, and felt fiercely ashamed, as if her untidiness was his fault.

'Nice lines she's got. He sail her much these days?'

'Hardly ever. He motors most of the time. She's got a Kelvin in her.'

'You going to take her over when you leave school, eh?' Sydney grinned at Gus, unaware that he was on a tender subject.

'No; he won't let me.' Gus started back along the sea-wall. 'He'll hardly let me set foot on her, else she wouldn't look such a shambles. Not if I had anything to do with her.'

Sydney, recognizing mutiny, did not continue with the subject. Much as he agreed with Gus's sentiments, he could hardly

concur in such filial undevotion. He knew Gus's father, Ted Roper, by sight and by hearsay, and much preferred what he knew of the son.

'She's had a hard life,' he excused her. 'How'd you fancy *Woodwind*, eh?'

'Oh, now she's a honey. A real yacht. I'd take her for a gift any day.'

The white yacht was laid up in a mud-berth, shrouded with canvas, but Gus was more than familiar with her lovely lines. In his estimation she raised the tone of Birdsmarsh harbour by several notches when she lay to her anchor in the channel.

'It's a pity there aren't a few more like her here,' he added.

'Well, you'll never get the general run of yachtsmen in a

place like this, that dries out,' Sydney said, with satisfaction. 'They'll stick to Mersea and Burnham. *Woodwind* belongs to a local man, doesn't she? Youngish chap? I've seen him aboard a few times.'

'Yes. Mr. Winnington up at the Research Station. I don't know him very well. He doesn't use her a lot.'

'You get old *Swansong* fitted out, and she'll look as sweet as any of your *Woodwinds*,' Sydney said. He saw no beauty in modern yachts, only in what he called 'little ships of character'. Gus thought him an old buffer in his point of view, but was in no position to argue.

'Well, *Swannie* should be all right, if we can rig her. She's sound, as far as I know.'

'She's not yours, you were saying?'

'No. She's Paul's.'

'Paul?'

'Paul Fairfax. His father owns all this.' Gus waved his hand vaguely over the sea-wall. 'She belonged to his uncle, but he died. Mr. Fairfax was going to sell her, but she hung on rather, and then Paul started using her as a sort of—well, den, I suppose you'd call it, so Mr. Fairfax forgot about her really. I think he more or less thinks of her as Paul's now, at any rate.'

'And Paul's keen to get her sailing now?'

'He will be, when I've brainwashed him a bit more. *I'm* keen to get her sailing, and Paul's bound to like it when he's tried it. He's a bit of a funny ass, in some ways. But all right,' he added. 'Absolutely all right.'

Sydney laughed. 'Poor Paul,' he said.

They plodded along in single file until they came to where *Swansong* lay. The tide had left her now, but she still sat upright, secure in the Blackwater mud. Sydney stood surveying her from the wall.

'She's a nice thing,' he said. 'The name rings a bell with me somewhere. Am I right in thinking she's the one the old boys call unlucky? Something about violent deaths aboard?'

'Yes, but it's a lot of rot. Her skipper during the war was shot dead on the foredeck by a German fighter—just bad luck on his part, because he was only fishing. Then Paul's uncle bought her after the war, and he died of a heart attack. He wasn't on board at the time, and he worked her without any trouble for years before it happened, so I honestly can't see that it makes her unlucky myself. I suppose it was just that he was youngish at the time, like the other skipper, and people want something to talk about.'

'Mmm, it's a shame to give a boat a name she doesn't deserve. In a place like this people are still superstitious. Has she got spars?'

'Yes. They're in the barn over at the farm. Quite good they are, too. And her mast's all right—topmast too. It's only sails and rigging she lacks.'

'As far as sails go, *Phoebe*'s got an old main I never use. It would just do her nicely. It's not too far gone. And I reckon I could find you a staysail. I don't know about a jib and topsail, though. I'll have to ask round the Society, or put an inquiry in our bulletin.'

'Main and staysail would do for a start,' Gus said eagerly, all his doubts falling gloriously away at Sydney's words. He felt as if *Swannie* were sailing out of her mud-berth before his very eyes. 'Really, if you could get us those, we could manage somehow. Even with the rigging.'

Sydney went aboard to take measurements, and Gus followed him round ecstatically. Sydney, for all his quaint ways, was a man after his own heart. He would talk boats without noticing time; he, of all the people Gus knew, appreciated how it felt to want to have a boat to sail, any old boat as long as she was seaworthy; how it was that one felt contented pottering on a boat; how it was that everything one did had meaning and sense. There was no mystique, no affectation, where boats were concerned. It was where Gus was on home ground. When he was feeling philosophical he supposed that this right feeling was because he came from generations of fishermen. Yet, ironically, because his father had missed out, he in whom the salt itch was so strong was to be denied by his father this natural, inborn thing which was all he wanted in life. He watched Sydney carefully measuring out the foredeck. Sydney was a Londoner born and bred, and was a doctor who came from generations of doctors, yet he knew *Swannie* as if he had built her with his own hands. Odd, Gus thought. Sometimes things didn't add up. He felt closer to Sydney that afternoon than he had ever felt to Paul.

'I'll sort the old mainsail out and bring it down next weekend,' Sydney said. 'And I reckon I could lay my hands on a staysail by then, too. New rigging, a bit of caulking and scrub her bottom, and you could have her sailing in a week or two.'

They sat on the hatch and discussed rigging. They went below and got the floorboards up and poked around in her bilges. Gus introduced the old engine, and they crouched against the thick frames in the cramped afterhold and talked of magnetos and timing. At four o'clock they went up on deck again and Sydney said it was time he was getting back.

'Paul said he might be down again after milking,' Gus said. It was beginning to go dusk already. 'I don't think he's coming, though. I'll walk back with you.'

The tide was right out, and the mud stretched away, shining and slaty to the grey water. Lights were beginning to come on in Mersea. They squelched across the saltings and up on to the sea-wall. As they climbed up, Paul appeared from the other side.

'Oh, I thought you weren't coming,' Gus said.

Paul looked at him as if he were a complete stranger. He was breathing hard, as if he had been hurrying; his face was white and he looked for all the world as if he had been crying. Gus stared at him.

'Whatever's wrong?'

But Paul had turned away, and set off at a run along the sea-wall in the opposite direction from the village. He ran wildly, all arms and legs, until he was well into the distance, while Gus stared after him in amazement.

'What's bitten him, for goodness' sake? He's acting crazy. He looked absolutely demented.'

'He looked distressed,' Sydney said. 'As if he's had a shock. Is he an excitable lad?'

'No. He's a dreamy nit most of the time.'

'Perhaps he's been in trouble at home, and wants to work it off,' Sydney said, glancing at his watch. 'I must be getting along. There are a few things I want to do aboard before it's dark. I didn't realize how the afternoon had gone.'

Gus followed Sydney along the sea-wall for a little way, but he couldn't help wondering what had got into Paul. The tight, wild face had shocked him. Paul was moody at times, but not as weird as all that. And he never got into trouble at home, not that sort of trouble. That was Gus's own prerogative. As they approached the harbour, he said to Sydney, 'I think I'll go back and see what Paul's up to. He's got me worried.'

'Yes, that a good idea,' Sydney said. 'I'll see you when I've got some sails, then.'

Gus hurried back the way he had come, half warm at the thought of a perfect afternoon and the parting promise, half curious about Paul. Paul wasn't on *Swannie*, although he had obviously been making for her when they met, and Gus guessed that he had gone on along the shore, turning to his favourite territory to be on his own. If Sydney hadn't been there, Gus thought Paul would have stayed. He hurried on anxiously. There was nothing but cold grey dusk ahead of him, and the smell of the North Sea and a rising wind. The shingle below the sea-wall gleamed white above the mud.

Paul was coming back, his hands in his pockets, kicking the line of flotsam under the wall. He saw Gus coming and stopped, looking up at him, but said nothing.

'What's up?' Gus asked. 'You've had me worried. I came back to see. Is something wrong?'

He skidded down the wall and Paul waited for him.

'What is it?' Gus said. He could see that Paul had been crying, and thought someone was dead.

'That—that man in the white Jaguar,' Paul said. 'He's buying up the farm.' He screwed a strip of seaweed into the shingle with the heel of his boot. 'They've been talking about it all day.'

'Buy it up? Whatever for? He wasn't a farmer, was he? Didn't look like one to me.'

'No, that's the point. He doesn't want to farm it. He——' Words failed Paul.

'He what? It's no good for anything else, surely?'

'He wants to build a marina on it. Flood all the western end and build lock-gates, berths for five hundred yachts, he said, and an hotel, and a car park for a thousand cars, and a swimming-bath and a club-house——' Paul choked.

Gus was stunned. He stared at Paul.

'Here? *Here?*'

Paul nodded.

Gus's sudden mental vision of the transformed Birdsmarsh took his breath away.

'He'll never do it, surely? Not really? I've heard of these ideas before. They never come to anything.'

'No? You should meet Mr. Glass,' Paul said bitterly.

'He looked stinking rich,' Gus remembered.

'He is. He's offered Dad far more than he'd ever get just selling as a farm. That's the trouble. And he's got the plans already roughed out. And the finance all arranged for carrying it out.'

'He's still got to get planning permission. That's what'll stop him.'

'Well, he doesn't seem to think so. He says it will bring work and trade here, and the County Council will like that. And if it comes to an appeal, he knows the Minister personally, he says. He's chosen the site with great care, he says, with planning permission particularly in mind. He says it's "all buttoned up".'

Gus looked at Paul uncertainly.

'These things take time, surely? Nothing's fixed, is it?'

'No. Only Dad's promised to go to London on Monday. To meet lawyers and things. It doesn't sound to me as if it will fall through. They've been talking all day, solid. Glass has got a list of references and credentials and big names and promises as long as your arm. It's not just a tin-pot little speculator. It's Glass, Roberts, Cohen, and Freeman of Mayfair. And some big-shot architect is going to design it. Dad's quite bowled over with the idea.'

'What about you?' Gus asked softly.

'What do *you* think?' Paul muttered. His voice was rough with tears.

'These schemes are being put on paper all the time, but not many come to anything,' Gus said. He hated to see Paul so distressed, yet another part of his mind, as if it were quite separate, was working away with a frantic, amazed excitement.

'Yes, Dad's still saying that, but he's all excited, just the same,' Paul said. 'He and Mum were talking like—like kids. About what they'd do with the money. I couldn't bear it. I wish Chris were home.'

'What do you think he'll say to it?'

'It won't affect him the same. But he—oh, he's got sense. He might help.'

Gus didn't see how. Chris had never been interested in the farm, only in getting into a university to study physics. A scholarship to Cambridge had removed him from the scene, and Gus doubted whether he felt any allegiance to Birdsmarsh now.

Paul shivered in the wind. He hadn't stopped to put a jacket on. 'I don't want to go home yet,' he said. 'Not to listen to it all.'

'Come home with me,' Gus said. 'Dad'll be going up the pub, and Mum won't mind.'

'I'll walk round your way. But don't say anything to anybody, will you?'

Paul could not tell Gus how he felt. The news had violated him to a degree where he felt completely stripped of any future content. He felt as if he were dangling in space. He could not conceive of his life without the farm. Another farm meant less than nothing to him. Birdsmarsh was his life. Birdsmarsh—that this fat, scented man was proposing to tarnish and tart up like Clacton sea front. He could not believe anything so bad could happen. He followed Gus along the sea-wall, shivering in the wind.

'Where's Paul gone?'

'I don't know. Wandering along the shore somewhere, I suppose.'

'Idiot child, to take it like that.'

'Did it surprise you? How did you expect him to take it?' Mrs. Fairfax looked at her husband impatiently for a moment. They were sitting by the fire in the living-room, too preoccupied even to pretend to knit or read.

'That's my reservation, in all this,' she said. 'Paul. He's a child of this place. It's just the way it is. It will be pulling him out by the roots. It's not the same for any of the rest of us. Chris won't bat an eyelid.'

'Nor will Paul when he sees the new farm this sort of money will buy.'

'He'll suffer a good deal first, though.'

'It's time he grew up,' Jim Fairfax said. 'Faced facts. He can't go on living in this—this dreamy sort of paradise of his all his life. Even if we go on here, he'll have to learn that farming is getting more of a factory business every day. God knows what sort of a farmer he's going to make, with his head in the clouds.'

'He's not fifteen till June,' Mrs. Fairfax pointed out. 'And you said the other day he was as good a cowman as any you've met. Doesn't that count for anything?'

'Yes, I won't deny it. He can deliver a tricky calf as well as the vet, in my opinion. But I'd like to see him sit down to that lot over there!' Mr. Fairfax waved his arm in the direction of an overflowing roll-top desk. 'He's a right dream at times, Lizzie, you can't deny it. We've as good as come up on the pools, and all he can do is look as if the sky's fallen in. I could have slapped him.'

'Give him time. He'll accept it when he's got used to the idea.'

'He's been too sheltered, that's his trouble. After all, knowing the way a cow works isn't going to make him a fortune, is it? But he doesn't seem to want to do anything else.'

'Why do you talk like that? It's been good enough for you, hasn't it? Most farmers would be pleased to have a son keen to carry on after them.'

'Yes, but even in farming you've got to have a bit of drive and ambition. Paul displays damn-all ambition, I must say. Here's the opportunity to start afresh, with better land, better buildings, to build up the herd, or, better still, go in for arable, with plenty of mechanization—that's where the future lies in farming today—and what's his reaction? Schoolgirl hysterics.'

'Don't exaggerate, Jim,' Mrs. Fairfax said sharply. 'Considering that you knocked his whole world from under his feet in a couple of sentences, I think he showed remarkable restraint. He's only a boy, for goodness' sake. Give him a bit of time.'

'Chris knew where he was going when he was fourteen.'

'Well, so does Paul. But he's quite different from Chris, you know that. He's always been quite content with the idea of taking over Birdsmarsh. You can't expect him to right-about-turn in five minutes. After all, the money means very little to him. I don't want to leave Birdsmarsh, come to that, but I can't pretend I'm not more than compensated by the thought of all that lovely money—if it comes off, of course.'

'Yes.' Jim Fairfax dismissed Paul from his mind and smiled. 'It's a marvellous thought. Let's keep our fingers crossed. You know, this news will shake the village when it's out.'

'If it comes off, it will mean big changes here. A lot of people won't like it.'

'Birdsmarsh has always been half a century behind the times. Buck its ideas up a bit.'

'Yes, but you're the one who stands to gain. I think, as far as the opposition is concerned, you'll be cast as the villain, not Mr. Glass.'

'I can stand it, with all that money behind me,' Jim Fairfax said happily. 'Things like this are happening all over. You can't stop them.' He didn't sound as if he wanted to.

His wife said nothing. If there were going to be differences of opinion about the plan for Birdsmarsh, which she guessed there were, her husband and son were going to represent the two extremes of thought. Up till now they had always got on amicably together. For herself, she knew what it was to come into money unexpectedly; however simple one's tastes and high-minded one's ideals, the sudden, glittering glimpse of unpremeditated fortune was bound to have an unnerving impact. Later, things would fall into perspective. But for now, she could not help feeling uneasy about Paul.

3
THE CONTENTS OF A SUITCASE

Paul sat beside his father in the Land-Rover and watched the bare twigs of the elms racing past. Easter was early, and the weather was still wintry, which fitted in well with his own frame of mind. They were going to meet Chris, and Paul was depending upon Chris to take sides with him, and point out to his father how the marina scheme would ruin Birdsmarsh.

'Not financially,' Gus had pointed out. Gus had said Chris would not care either way what happened to Birdsmarsh, but Paul could not believe it would mean so little. Chris had brains, and their father took notice of Chris's opinions, which was more than he did of Paul's. Paul glowered at the passing landscape. In his mind's eye he saw the yachtsmen flashing past to the marina, their horrible children running along his own beach, flushing up the sheldrake chicks. His father was humming 'Rule Britannia' out of tune. The lawyers had told him that the Birdsmarsh marina scheme was very sound. Finance was available and it only needed the necessary permissions from the county planning departments to go ahead.

'What time is that train due in?' Jim Fairfax asked, glancing at his watch.

'Two thirty something. Can't remember exactly.'

They drove into the station yard just as the diesel train came bustling into the terminus. The diesel train, five miles from Birdsmarsh, was its most tangible link with civilization. London lay an hour and a half away, with one change. Comparative accessibility to London was one of Mr. Glass's favourite themes. Paul looked at the efficient two-coach diesel sourly. Not that the Birdsmarsh yachtsmen would use it, he thought. They would come in Rolls-Royces, to fit in with Mr. Glass's flash hotel, sun-lounges (even Mr. Glass wouldn't be able to guarantee the sun), hairdressing saloons and restaurants. ('Although, if they've got yachts, what will they be wasting time hanging around in that lot for?' Gus had asked.) Paul followed his father on to the platform.

The train came to a halt and Chris got out right opposite them.

'Hullo, Dad. Hullo, Paul. How's things?'

'Nice to have you back again, Chris. No female this time, eh?'

'Oh, God, no. I've given up females since Amanda. Hi, wait a minute.'

A porter was slamming the doors shut, and Chris dived back into the train, to emerge with an enormous, very battered and disreputable-looking suitcase. He had already taken out his ordinary suitcase with his initials on that he usually travelled with, and both Paul and his father looked at the extra luggage with surprise.

'Good heavens! Have you left Cambridge for good?' Mr. Fairfax said.

'No. It's just some—some work I'm in the middle of. Want to get on with it during the vac.' Chris looked as if he didn't want to discuss it.

'I'll bring the cow truck next time,' Mr. Fairfax said with a grin.

They trailed out to the Land-Rover. Paul took the large suitcase and found it quite light. He was curious, but said nothing. Seeing Chris again, it was almost as if he had never been away. His manner was so easy; he never changed. He was always affable and kind. Paul wished he could be like Chris. To look at, they were alike. Chris was tall and fair, better-looking than Paul, but with the same eyes (only his could see better) and the same lean figure. It might have been described as athletic, save that neither of them had ever been keen on sport. Chris was tidy and methodical, which showed in his appearance. Apart from his work, his only interest was in music.

They put the suitcases in the back and squeezed into the Land-Rover. Paul sat in the middle. As soon as his father had driven out of the station yard, Chris brought up the inevitable subject.

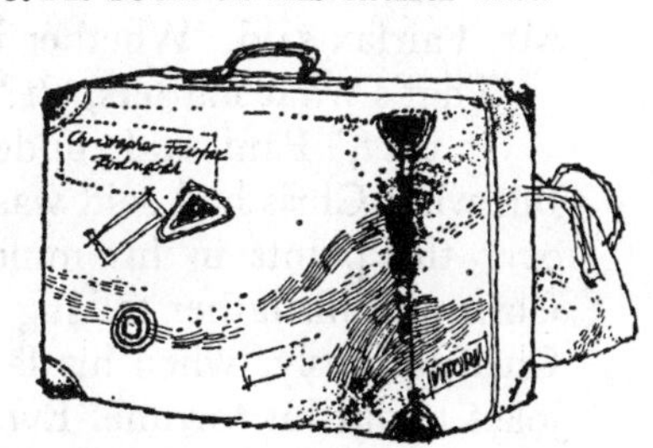

'Next time I come it'll be a Rolls to meet me, then?'

Jim Fairfax laughed.

'Keep your fingers crossed, lad. Seems like we might be in the money.'

'It came as a bit of a surprise, didn't it? I must say I was astonished when I read Mother's letter. Birdsmarsh, of all the back-of-beyond places! It's the last place you'd have thought the speculators would hit upon.'

'Well, not when it comes to these marina things. Handy spot for sailing from.'

'I can't see why they can't dredge the harbour and make moorings that way.'

'Even with dredging, there'd be no water in it when the tide's out. This marina thing has lock-gates, he was telling us. You can get in and out at all states of the tide.'

'I reckon that'll be some engineering feat. Have you seen any details of how they plan to do it?'

'No. Don't know if they know themselves yet.'

'Hm.' Chris sounded sceptical.

'Why?' said Paul eagerly. 'Don't you think it's possible?'

'Yes, it's possible; but it strikes me that it might be very expensive to do efficiently. That means that the yachtsmen are going to have to pay a lot of money for their moorings if the man behind the business is going to make something from it.'

'Well, he's not doing it for love of the poor British yachtsman, I can tell you. Not our Mr. Glass.' Jim Fairfax chuckled.

'Do you think there's any chance that it might not happen?' Paul asked Chris.

'Oh, yes,' Chris replied. 'They might not get planning permission, for a start. Then, if they do, they might find it's more complicated to do than they imagined. And then there's the question of raising money. Even if they say now that the finance is all ready and waiting, when it comes to the point it might not all be quite so easy. I can see plenty of snags.'

'We'll wait and see. The man has guaranteed an option,' Mr. Fairfax said. 'Whether it comes off or whether it doesn't.'

'That's what matters, eh?' Chris said, smiling.

'It isn't,' Paul said, under his breath. No one heard him. But what Chris had said was something of a comfort. He went over the points in his mind as the journey continued, with Chris and his father talking across him. Later he would talk to Chris seriously, when his father wasn't there to keep making jokes about his fortune. Ever since Mr. Glass had called, Paul had hated his father for his vulgar preoccupation with money. His father had called Paul a 'long-haired prig', and Mrs. Fairfax had had her work cut out keeping the atmosphere free of animosity. She was still giving Paul time to settle down to the idea of selling Birdsmarsh, but Jim Fairfax reckoned he had had all the time he ought to need.

When they got home Paul lugged the enormous suitcase out of the back of the Land-Rover. Chris said to him, 'Will you take it up to my room and stuff it under the bed? I don't want Mum to start asking questions. I'll tell you about it later.' He spoke softly, so that Mr. Fairfax did not hear. Paul was warmed by the confidence, and as he carried the case upstairs felt more cheerful than he had for days. Chris coming home always gave the house a holiday feel; his mother was laughing in the kitchen and the kettle was clattering its lid on the stove, ready for one of the innumerable cups of tea that were made during the day. Chris had been relegated to the smaller bedroom since he had left home and Paul had taken over Chris's old room, so that he could use Chris's record-player. 'The Monster', Mrs. Fairfax called it, when she stepped over the conglomeration of boxes, wires and speakers. The record-player was in a constant state of 'being improved' and had never reached the stage of being tidily shut away in walnut veneer, nor was it ever likely to. Both boys doted on it, and Mrs. Fairfax was not houseproud enough to object to it. Apart from the record-player, Paul much preferred his new room, as it looked out over the marshes instead of along the drive to the village. Like most of the rooms in the house, the floor was uneven and the ceiling ran slightly downhill. It creaked, and when the wind blew fierce draughts came in through the small window. Mrs. Fairfax was already talking about modern bungalows with oil-fired central heating.

Paul shoved the big case under the bed. It rattled in a loose, muffled fashion. He wondered why Chris was going to talk to him about it. Usually Chris's work was completely unintelligible to the rest of the family and he never spoke about it at home. Out of the window the marshes were bright with new grass, and the Friesians were strung out like a necklace of black and white beads.

Paul went downstairs and his father told him to go and start the milking. Chris's being home made no difference to the work to be done; Paul had hardly ever been away from the farm with his family and had never known the meaning of a 'family holiday'. In the summer he sometimes went to cousins in Northamptonshire, but he was always glad to get home. Chris had never helped much on the farm, and Paul knew he would sit in the kitchen drinking tea and talking to his mother while the work outside went on as it always did, animals calling the tune to the farmer as the tides did to the fishermen. Paul loved the irrevocable rhythm of farming, the day-after-day culture of the unmoved cow, who ate her grass and chewed her cud and gave her milk and slept. Chris called it boiler-stoking, the work his father did, and said it would drive him round the bend, but Paul found it completely satisfying. Chris said it was archaic, that it could all be done by machinery, even milk could be processed without cows. He said the Birdsmarsh fishermen were a hundred years out of date, and the farmers fifty. Paul thought about this as he let the cows in, but it didn't make any difference. He didn't mind being fifty years out of date.

Later, after tea, Chris picked up his other case and said, 'Well, I'll take my things up.' He looked at Paul and nodded upstairs with his head. Paul took the hint and followed him.

'Where did you put that case?' Chris asked him when they were on the landing.

'In my room, under the bed. What is it?'

'I'll show you in a minute.'

Chris opened the door of Paul's old room, flung his case in and then followed Paul into the bigger room. He shut the door and looked round approvingly.

'You know that old boat in the saltings?' he said unexpectedly. 'That one of Uncle Arthur's? Is she still afloat?'

'Why, yes.' Paul looked up in surprise. It was the first time anyone in the family had mentioned *Swannie* for years.

'Is she in working order? I mean, could we take her out into the river without committing suicide?' Chris asked.

'How funny you should ask,' Paul said. 'We're just doing her up now. She's got a new suit of sails and Gus has got her engine going. We were going to take her out for a trial run on Saturday.'

Chris nodded. 'That's the best bit of news I've heard for a long time,' he said. 'I was afraid she would have fallen to bits by now.'

'But whatever do you want her for?' Paul asked. 'Have you taken up sailing or something?'

'No. I want to do some trials on the water, and I've got to have a boat as a base. That old thing will suit me fine.'

Chris looked at Paul thoughtfully. He was leaning on one of the stereo speakers on the window-sill, his face very serious, almost drawn, in a way Paul could remember seeing when he used to do his homework at the kitchen table.

'Trials? What sort of trials?'

'It's this thing I've got in the suitcase.' Chris came across the room and groped under the bed. 'It's what I've been working on for the last year. All I think about, most of the time.' He pulled the suitcase out and knelt beside it, and Paul, sitting on the bed, looked down at its dilapidated lid anxiously.

'Why? What is it?'

'I hope it's going to make me a fortune,' Chris said. Paul had never seen Chris so unflippant about his work before. There was not the suspicion of a joke in his voice, and his eyes were positively loving as he slid back the locks. 'If only I can get it to stand a real test—and I reckon that will be in about two or three months' time—when I can, then I shall really have something, Paul.'

Paul leaned over as Chris lifted the lid. He didn't know what he expected to see, but Chris's manner intrigued him. The suitcase was filled with a limp black rubber material and sundry bits of tubing and straps and buckles and zip-fasteners. Paul wasn't at all impressed, but his eyes showed genuine curiosity.

'Looks like a frogman's suit,' he said.

'It's an exposure suit,' Chris said. 'There's a difference. Look.' He pulled the suit out and laid it on the floor. 'You see, there are two layers. One layer lies next to the skin. The gap between is filled with air, and divided by bulkheads into several compartments. You inflate the thing with this air canister here, via this valve on the chest. Air enters the compartments through a one-way valve. Once it's in, that's it, barring punctures. The air, besides keeping you afloat, keeps you warm, and the bulkheads ensure that it's kept all round you, instead of shooting topsides and leaving the back without insulation.'

'But——' Paul stared at the strange object. Whatever he might have expected, it certainly wasn't this. 'You mean, you invented it? Or you made it? Or what? This isn't what you do at Cambridge, is it? I thought you went to lectures and things.'

Chris smiled. 'Yes, I do. But, you see, there are facilities there for doing all manner of things, and you get interested in something, you get talking to someone, and ideas get planted, and in my case it led to this. It started as just an idea.' He looked at it thoughtfully. It was certainly more than an idea now; Paul felt that it had a presence all its own, lying there between them like an empty, robot man, asprawl, slightly grotesque. 'We call it Charlie,' Chris added. This was a statement, still not a joke.

'You made it?'

'Yes. Not all on my own, of course. There's a bloke called Proctor, whose father has worked in marine equipment. He helped in quite a lot of ways. Proctor's in on it, of course. But the idea and the design are mine and, when it's ready, it will be patented in my name. First, though, it's got to be tested. That's where the old boat comes in.'

'You're going to test it? Get in it, I mean, and go floating about?'

'Yes.'

'It's safe, then?'

'Of course, nitwit. It's a life-saving suit.' Chris smiled, at last. 'All the same, I'd rather Mum and Dad didn't know about it just yet. I can make out I've got interested in sailing or fishing or some such, and we can keep Charlie on the boat.' He paused, and considered the suit once more. 'Eventually, you see, when it's ready, I want to give it a real working out, at least twenty-four hours off shore, more if possible. Proctor thinks we could rig it with a little sail eventually, but I haven't got round to such refinements yet. It's still in a very basic stage yet. There are quite a few problems to be worked out.'

Paul had never seen Chris in the light of an inventor before. This offspring of his amazed him. Chris's attitude, too, was new to Paul; he realized that he was seeing a side of Chris that he had never appreciated before. He had always known that Chris was brainy, but it had never really showed, as far as Paul could remember. He had never carried on learned conversations or pored over heavy tomes (except in the privacy of his own room); he was never pompous, nor had he ever shown any signs of being bored with his rustic family, in spite of their being fifty years out of date. At home he had always been funny and teasing and rather lazy. But now there was a look in his eye Paul had never seen before. It was rather like Gus's when he had helped Sydney bend on *Swannie*'s new sails. Paul realized, quite suddenly, that Chris, to whose homecoming he had so looked forward, would only be concerned with the fate of Birdsmarsh in so far as it affected his plans for testing his suit. In competition with Charlie, the problem of Birdsmarsh and Mr. Glass would mean nothing to him.

A bitter disappointment seized Paul as Chris started to fold his suit tenderly back into the case. Nobody in the world cared about Birdsmarsh being turned into a marina, Chris least of all. Chris, aware of his brother's withdrawal, looked up from the floor and, misinterpreting, said, 'It's all right my borrowing that old smack? You'll help me with this, will you? I'm not going to mess up any of your plans?'

'Oh, no,' Paul said hastily. 'Of course not. Gus'll be jolly interested in all this.'

'You can tell Gus about it, of course, but don't talk about it to anyone else. It's not that it's a secret, just that I'd rather Mum doesn't know what I'm doing. It's not a bit dangerous, of course, but I'll never get her to see that. When do you think we'll be able to get started?'

'Any time after Saturday, if she goes all right, I suppose. We've got three weeks off school and I think Gus was planning to use it all on *Swannie*, so I don't see why we can't do your trials at the same time.'

'That would suit me fine.'

Chris started to sort through the box of records that stood on the chest of drawers. He took one out and put it on the turntable. Paul knew that it was going to be Beethoven's Seventh Symphony before any noise came out of the speakers at all, and he went and leaned on the window-sill and looked out across the empty fields. It was raining, which suited the way he felt. The estuary was grey and the grey clouds looked as if they were resting on the water. Pools gleamed in the fields; the ditches were brimming and the gateways black with churned mud. Chris did not know it, would not see it even if his eyes went to the window. He was lying on the bed, waving one foot to the music, which was very loud. His eyes were full of a sensuous pleasure at his favourite noise, and his mind was roving with a contented anticipation, warm with excitement at his achievement and the plans to be followed up. Paul could sense his perfect content. He stood with his back to the room, watching the rain running down the thick uneven glass and listening to the great rhythmic melodies that filled the room, and hating every moment that he stood there. Whatever Chris might have to say about Birdsmarsh, now or in the future, Paul knew would only be words, meaningless and comfortless, because he thought less than nothing about what happened there. But if he was to talk about his suit, his ridiculous, useless, grotesque mummy of limp rubber cloth, his heart would be in his eyes and he would feel and speak as strongly and with the same purpose as Paul would talk about Birdsmarsh if there was anyone prepared to listen to him. But Paul had found out that there was nobody who felt the same as he did about Mr. Glass's proposition. There was no one who shared his wild feeling of outrage for his precious shore; nobody else did more than lift their eyebrows and ask questions about the money. Paul knew that his father thought he was mad, and his mother was losing patience, and that Gus, even Gus, wanted the marina to happen, although he hadn't actually said so.

'Chris,' he said.

Chris didn't hear him. Paul wanted to say it again, but the music had swelled up with a crescendo of urgent brass. Paul looked out at the rain again. 'All you think of is yourself,' his father had said, and Paul thought with a wild indignation, 'Why pick on me?' Chris was just the same, and Gus and Sydney and Mr. Glass and Jim Fairfax himself, all thinking about the things that affected their own lives, personally. He was no worse. The magnificent noise filled the room, triumphantly cascading melodies raining on his gloom. Paul thought, 'Beethoven was deaf when he wrote this. He never heard it,' and realized that there were tragedies in life beyond his comprehension. He was on the fringe of a little trouble, no doubt. But it felt like the whole world.

4

TRIALS ON 'SWANNIE'

'Make fast the staysail sheet!'

'What on earth is the staysail sheet?' Chris asked Paul.

'Don't ask me. I think it's that rope flapping about there.'

Chris pulled experimentally.

'That's it. Round that cleat,' Gus said. He stood at the tiller, trying not to look excited. The patched mainsail strained sweetly above his head to a light south-westerly wind as *Swannie* made out on a broad reach across the river. She had come alive; Gus could feel her working under his feet, the old seams weeping and the caulking giving, the gaff jaws creaking gently in amazement at their new lease of life. 'You old thing,' he was saying to her in his mind, 'you lovely old hulk. Who said you couldn't go?' The curve of her laid decks stretching out before him from under his feet gave him a thrill he had never experienced before. The feel of her, pulling and yet giving to his hand on the tiller, made him feel like God. Ashamed of his sentiment, he kept his face very non-committal. He stood with his feet squarely planted on the flat deck, the collar of his donkey jacket pulled up, his dark eyes trying to look critical.

Chris and Paul sat with their backs to the afterhatch. It was cold and they neither of them had any idea of what to do. This worried Paul, but Chris was looking at the flat sturdy deck of the old smack, so low to the water at the stern, and thinking how admirably she would suit his purpose. She was virtually a sailing platform for the fishermen to work their nets on; the deck was uncomplicated by the normal yacht's cockpit, coamings, cabin-top and guard-rails, and he would be able to get in and out over the bulwarks without any trouble. He was astounded by his luck in having *Swannie* all ready and at hand, with a crew to work her. Paul was willing, if nothing else, but Gus was practical and reliable beyond his years when it came to boats. Chris put his hands in his pockets and started to whistle.

Paul, recognizing the slow movement of Beethoven's Seventh, remembered his disappointment in Chris, and hunched himself sourly into the hood of his anorak. To see Gus standing there, confident and trying not to look too pleased with himself, and to hear Chris whistling at his side, made Paul aware that he was the only one unappreciative of *Swannie*'s renaissance. He looked down at the water sweeping past her heaving bulwarks and tried to pretend that he liked sailing. The deck felt nervous and alive beneath him, nothing like the erstwhile solid roof of his own private den. The water was so close as to look positively dangerous, even leaping at intervals in a scuffle of spray along the lee deck. He felt cold and uncomfortable and useless.

'Want to take her?' Gus offered generously.

Paul shook his head. 'Not yet.'

He felt slightly sick, if the truth were known, which made him hate the whole business even more.

'Have you told Gus that I want to use *Swannie* this holiday?' Chris asked him.

He shook his head.

Chris started to tell Gus about his suit, and Paul looked back at the shore and visualized the sun-lounge sticking up above the sea-wall, the forest of masts behind some massive and hideous lock-gates, and a welter of outboard motors coming and going off the shingle. Even as it was now, unspoilt, his shore looked unfamiliar from this angle. It was an insignificant shore from the water, a mere hardening of the horizon where the sea-wall stood up, with nothing beyond to disturb the grey clouds save a pair of wheeling curlews. It was strange, Paul thought, that for all the years he had known it he had rarely seen it from the sea. Boats had never had any attraction for him, and he felt no reason now to change his opinion.

As Gus wanted to leave the smack in the harbour now that she was officially sailing—'Just during the holidays,' he said hastily. 'She can go back in her old berth afterwards.'—they had to wait till high water to get in.

'Now, if we had a marina,' he said to Paul, too full of high spirits to be tactful, 'we could steam in whenever we wanted.'

It was dusk by the time they dropped anchor in the channel behind *Phoebe*. Sydney hailed them and rowed alongside in his dinghy. Paul had already got the stove going, slightly surprised to find that one could have a cheerful fire below even when the boat was batting along through an uneasy sea; the lamp cast its greenish glare over the tidy cabin and the kettle steamed spasmodically on top of the stove. Paul had to admit that actually sailing the boat had done no harm; in fact, he had a feeling that *Swannie* was pleased with herself, back in her element. He liked the harsh rasp of the anchor chain as it ran up through the hawse and the slap of water in the bilges, and, now that they had stopped, he decided that sailing wasn't really so bad.

Sydney came down the companion-way, beaming and appreciative. Gus introduced Paul and Chris and they all sat down, fitting their heads carefully between the deck beams. Paul started rooting about for the teapot, feeling that he must make an effort to assert himself as *Swannie*'s owner in face of the technical talk that was passing across the table between Gus and Sydney. By the time he had found four chipped cups and a packet of damp sugar, one bent teaspoon and a tin of rather mouldy tea, the conversation had changed to a subject nearer his own heart.

'Someone's been telling me there's talk of a marina being built here,' Sydney said. 'Is it true? Do you know anything about it?'

'Oh, yes, it's true,' Gus said cheerfully. 'Ask Paul. He'll tell you.'

'Kettle's boiling,' Chris said. 'Is the tea in the pot?'

'Yes,' Paul said.

Chris reached over for the kettle.

'The scheme has been proposed,' he said to Sydney, 'but it's got a long way to go before it's accepted.'

'But the proposition is genuine?' Sydney said. 'It's got money behind it, I presume? Not just some local landowner's bright idea for making himself a fortune?'

'Oh, yes, it's a sound scheme,' Chris said. 'But whether it will get planning permission is another matter.'

'Where is it going?' Sydney persisted. 'I gather it's not going to be anything to do with the harbour?'

'Over the sea-wall where *Swannie* was lying,' Paul said. 'They're going to make a basin behind the sea-wall. On our land—Father's land, at least. But it wasn't his idea,' he felt forced to admit. 'It's these London people's idea.'

Sydney opened his mouth to voice his opinion of 'these London people', then remembered that he was at that moment a guest of the family that stood to benefit.

'Well, these things happen . . .' he said heavily.

'I don't see why they should!' Paul said vehemently. 'We don't want it. Father would never have thought of such a thing, either, if they hadn't come down with all their filthy money and towny ideas.'

'Steady on, Paul,' Chris said.

'It's true. Why, do *you* want it?' Paul turned angrily on Chris. 'You don't care because you don't live here any more. But I care. It was going to be my farm. If I had my way, I'd tell them what to do with their stupid plans. Spoiling *our* place, using it. It means nothing to them, shoving concrete and car parks into a back-of-beyond place like Birdsmarsh in order to line their own pockets.'

Chris looked surprised.

'But there'll be enough to buy a new farm,' he said. 'And you can't say this is a pretty place. What are they spoiling? These things are happening everywhere. People want to sail these days—look at us—so naturally there has to be somewhere to pack all the boats. What's so sinful about it?'

Sydney said eagerly, 'I must say, I agree with Paul. I think it's shameful importing such an urban idea as a marina into an unspoilt stretch of coast like this. If they must have them, why can't they put them in places that are spoilt already? I was aghast when I heard of this plan.'

'With all due respect, sir'—Chris was obviously going to be rude—'you like this place, why shouldn't other people enjoy it too?'

'Because when it's full of other people there will be no peace and quiet to enjoy,' Paul butted in. 'Dr. Peacemaker likes it how I do.'

Sydney smiled. 'Yes, I do. I know it's a selfish attitude, but after all, I'm quite prepared to put up with the drawbacks. The mud, for example, and the difficulties of getting in and out when you want, and the lack of facilities. I'd rather have it that way, and have the place to myself, than be molly-coddled in a yacht-basin along with four hundred others.'

Chris nodded. 'I see your point, of course. I'd feel the same myself. Only it is a thing we've got to face now, increasingly. There will have to be provision made for people's recreation, now that with motor-cars they have become so mobile.'

'Chris, you sound like a newspaper,' Paul said disgustedly. 'What's that got to do with Birdsmarsh? Mr. Glass doesn't give a damn about the poor people wanting recreation. He only wants to make a lot of money.'

'Obviously he's not doing it for a hobby,' Chris said. 'But there are so many sides to this thing, Paul. It's your farm, your land, and you're indignant, but he's offered you more than adequate compensation.'

'Money can't buy everything,' Paul said. 'You're as bad as Father. Money makes everything right, he thinks. Well, I don't think so.'

'That's because you've never wanted for it,' Gus said suddenly. 'It's easy for you to talk.'

Paul glowered at Gus. 'Yes, I know you want it to happen. You haven't said so, but I could see it in your face when I told you about it.'

'It might give me work, that's all I'm worried about. The sort of work I want,' Gus said. 'You see it your way; I see it mine. It's natural.'

'We're all concerned according to how it affects us,' Sydney said. 'My attitude is probably the most selfish of all, as Chris pointed out. I'm here and I like it, so keep all the other people out so that I can enjoy it on my own. Well, I'm old, and I'm not ashamed.'

'What's the local attitude?' Chris asked Gus. 'For or against?'

'Both,' Gus said. 'Everybody's been nattering about it, but it doesn't add up to much. I think the Council are for it, though.'

'Yes, they would be,' Chris said. 'They'll be hoping a marina will solve all their problems. But the county planners might turn it down.'

'Even if they do,' Sydney said, 'the developer can appeal, I suppose. To the Ministry.'

'There would be an inquiry,' Chris agreed, 'and a whole lot of long-haired cranks in plus-fours will descend on the place and start declaiming about the nesting sites of the lesser piebald song-thrush——'

'I hope you're not including me amongst the turn-out,' Sydney remarked, smiling.

'Of course,' Chris said, grinning back. 'They'll all be from London, like you, and no one in Birdsmarsh will have set eyes on any of them.'

Sydney laughed. 'I think I'm well enough known round here. All the locals think the Smack Preservation Society is just about the funniest thing that's ever happened. They choke into their beer up at the pub every time I go through the door. That's so, isn't it, Gus?'

Gus, startled, looked embarrassed. 'Oh, no—er—not really——'

Sydney looked sad again. 'Oh, yes, it's true, but I don't mind. I know I'm a backward old fool, and I know that I ought to move with the times, but I'm afraid I can't get interested in fibre-glass yachts and marinas and what-have-you.'

'Nor can I, especially in Birdsmarsh,' Paul said.

'Let's have some tea,' Chris said. 'It'll be stewed.'

Afterwards, when they were walking home along the sea-wall, Chris said to Paul, 'I didn't know you felt like that about this scheme. Mum said you'd been a bit upset, but I didn't realize you were so dead set against it.'

'It's all I think about,' Paul muttered. 'It's ruined everything.'

'I suppose it's come at an unfortunate time, just when you're about ready to start work. I suppose Dad will stay on until the plans are either given the go-ahead or turned down, which might take some time. It leaves you rather unsettled.'

'It's not just that. I don't want it to happen. Even if we go away and start afresh I shall keep thinking about it, back here. Spoilt. It's my place. I can't think of any other.'

Chris grimaced to himself in the dusk. His imagination didn't work the same way as Paul's. He looked along the sea-wall and saw the dark saltings standing up below them, the ebb sucking out through the narrow channels with a sad echo, and the pale line of the shingle farther on where the wall turned southward. Out by the water some waders were making eerie, wavering, evening noises. It was, he supposed, an attractive place in its negative way; he appreciated that it could get into a person's bones—a person like Paul, who was a solitary, reserved person. He glanced sideways at Paul's profile, set in a childish sulk, and yet not childish in the line of the jaw and the firmness of his lips. Chris saw the stubbornness which angered his father, and the vulnerability it covered. It was useless to try to comfort such an attitude with mere sympathy. It was a thing Paul was going to have to work out on his own.

Chris shrugged in the darkness and started thinking about his suit.

Paul worried about Chris. It was all very well saying that the thing wasn't dangerous, but it wasn't easy to keep an eye on the seal-like black figure drifting on the tide down a sour, wave-topped March estuary.

'Rather him than me,' Gus said, blowing on his numb fingers as he stood at the tiller. *Swannie* was under power, making big circles to stay in the same vicinity as Chris.

'It must work all right,' Paul said, glancing at his watch. 'He's been in over an hour now and seems quite happy. And the water must be freezing. I wish we could see him more easily, though.'

'If we lost him it wouldn't matter much, if the suit's all right. He's only got to swim to the shore. It's a darned clever idea.'

'He's hoping it's going to make him a fortune,' Paul said.

Gus grinned. 'Your family's certainly going to be in the money!'

Paul was unamused. He grunted crossly. He was shivering and anxious.

'If we're going to do much of this,' he said, 'I think we ought to make him tow a yellow buoy or something.'

'We'll go close and see if he's had enough,' Gus said. He put the tiller over and added, 'I have.'

As *Swannie* closed with Chris the two boys could see that, far from looking as if he were anxious for rescue, he was lying relaxed on his back, his hands behind his head, singing one of the innumerable stanzas of 'The Golden Vanity'.

'How's things?' Paul bawled over the racket of the engine.

'Fine.'

'Are you coming aboard?'

Chris started to paddle towards the smack. He was a strong swimmer, and had swum across the estuary when he was Paul's age. Gus throttled down, and Chris came alongside the counter. His face, framed in the closely fitting black hood, was not as pinched with cold as Paul's; it glowed with well-being. With Paul's help he clambered on board. Gus grinned at him from the tiller.

'Looks like something out of the circus,' he said.

'Pneumatic man,' Chris said. 'The one and only.' He released a valve and the fat, dimpled suit deflated all round him, leaving him looking like a skin-diver in a suit too big for him.

'It works all right. I'm as warm as toast,' he said.

'More than we are,' Gus said.

Chris undid a zip down his chest and pushed the hood back.

His thick straw-coloured hair was flattened damply to his head; his eyes shone with an excitement he was too sophisticated to want to reveal to the younger boys.

'That's the first time I've had it in real conditions. At least, nearer real conditions than before. We borrowed a private swimming-pool at Cambridge.'

Paul helped him peel off the two linked layers of the suit. Underneath he was wearing a pair of long woollen combinations and a sweater. Gus watched thoughtfully from the tiller. It was an undeniably cold day and the water was wintry, yet Chris was obviously quite comfortable. Gus was impressed, and curious.

'What's it for, this suit?' he asked. 'Who's going to buy the idea?'

'The Government, I hope.' Chris buckled his trouser belt and shrugged into a shabby anorak. 'At the moment, anyone who finds himself in the drink—a pilot, say, who's had to bale out—has no chance of surviving in northern waters unless he's picked up almost at once. Even in the North Sea they reckon twenty minutes in winter is enough to kill you. In Arctic waters it's far less, of course. The ultimate purpose is to make this suit comfortable enough for anyone working in cold waters to wear as a matter of course. Trawlermen apart, there are plenty of potential customers in the goings-on of the Defence Ministry. It could become a normal part of the gear for reconnaissance in the Arctic, or for anything a bit risky in small boats, submarines or what have you. There's definitely a market for it, if it turns out all right.'

He picked up the suit and hung it carefully over the boom to dry off in the cold breeze. Gus headed *Swannie* for the harbour and said, 'If you're in it for a long time, at sea, what happens when you want to—'

'Oh, we've solved that one,' Chris said happily. 'It was tricky, though.' He turned the suit over on its back, and showed them what looked like a sleeve, neatly rolled up, between the two legs. 'You see, you can lift this opening up clear of the surface and put in a bottle or something, which will be part of the kit eventually. Then you can empty it and roll this up again out of the way.'

'That's cunning,' Paul said, impressed. He knew now that

Chris's suit was a professional piece of work, something that Chris had every justification for being absorbed in. He no longer felt impatient and disappointed in Chris, but involved in his business whether he liked it or not.

'If these first trials go off without a hitch, we'll have to make plans for a proper one. At least twenty-four hours.' Chris sat on the edge of the hold, the gleam still in his eye. 'It's a pity it won't be January, but even in April a period as long as that should prove it fairly satisfactorily. Well off shore, of course.'

'I don't know if *Swannie*'d be the boat for that,' Gus said doubtfully. 'You'd want something pretty reliable.'

'I don't know. Proctor's idea in rigging up a sail on the thing is that we could make a North Sea crossing without a boat standing by at all. Now, that would be something.'

Paul stared. 'Suicide, I'd say.'

'I don't think the sail is very practicable myself, but it might work out later. It's worth bearing in mind.'

Paul shrugged. He wondered what his mother would say if she could overhear the conversation. Gus was throttling *Swannie* down to nose up the narrow channel into Birdsmarsh. There was an hour to go to high water. Small sullen waves slapped busily on the mud banks on either side and a pair of cormorants flew across their bows and went skimming out to sea.

'Look,' Gus said suddenly, 'Mr. Winnington's got *Woodwind* out on the water. She would do for your trials, Chris, if you had a chat with him. She's got a new diesel in her. Suit you fine.'

'What's he like?' Chris asked.

'Winnington? Seems all right. Keeps himself to himself rather. I don't know him very well. But he doesn't mind going off shore. He goes to Holland quite a lot. Dr. Peacemaker, now, is a creek potterer. I don't think he'd be much good for what you want.'

The two boats, *Phoebe* and *Woodwind*, lay on their moorings ahead, the sleek white yacht and the tidy black smack. To Gus they were like a moral illustration of all he felt about boats and life in general: the feeling came to him quite suddenly, looking at them and judging where to put *Swannie* so that she wouldn't give either of them a foul berth. *Woodwind* was clean and modern and efficient: he admired her desperately. But *Phoebe* was merely a well-kept anachronism, a true symbol of Birdsmarsh itself and its stick-in-the-mud ways. *Swannie*'s keel kissed the mud and the old engine coughed touchily, and Gus put the tiller over and longed with all his heart for Mr. Glass's yacht-harbour to transform Paul's dreary marshes and inject a little life into the obsolete village.

5
CHRIS IN TROUBLE

Once the novelty of Chris's experiments had worn off, Gus and Paul took their duties rather more carelessly, inspired by Chris's confidence. Once they had dropped him overboard they would carry on, some way down tide of him, and wait at anchor. Paul took the precaution of keeping an eye on him with the binoculars at intervals, while Gus got on with some job on the rigging or engine. It wasn't the way they would have chosen to spend their time on *Swannie*, but they both of them thought Chris's work was important enough to merit their support. Besides, Chris was satisfied with his trials, having decided what small modifications were needed, and told them a week later, 'One more. Then we can start thinking about the real thing. I'll go back to Cambridge and get Proctor to start making some arrangements. He's good at organizing people.'

'We ought to take some fish home,' Paul said to Gus, as they sat on the hatch, waiting. 'Mother thinks that's what we do all day. She's beginning to think we're rotten.'

'I'll get some off my father,' Gus said. 'Did you notice *Woodwind* had gone, by the way? They say she went out on the tide Wednesday night.'

'Where to?'

'I don't know. I wouldn't mind a sail on her, some time. I wonder if he's ever short of crew?'

'Ask him.'

Gus shrugged. 'He'd think it a cheek, I imagine.'

Paul picked up the binoculars. 'I saw a bar-tailed godwit yesterday over the sea-wall.'

'It's a swimming Fairfax you're on the look-out for.'

Paul surveyed the grey water intently. It was choppy and cold with gleams of sunlight far out at sea, and the trees on Mersea were still brown and bare. The strong spring tide was flooding. They had dropped Chris off the Bench Head buoy, which Paul could see through the binoculars, about a mile away.

'He should be pretty near by now,' Gus said.

'I can't see him.'

Gus stood up. He frowned, staring out over *Swannie*'s bows. 'A little to your left,' he said, glancing at Paul. 'There's something, but it looks——'

'Yes,' Paul said. 'But——' He hesitated, then passed the binoculars to Gus. 'You have a look. He looks submerged to me. Sort of head down.'

There was a restrained urgency in his voice. He didn't want to seem frightened, knowing that he was a nervous coot compared with Gus, and that Chris was always scoffing at his worries. Gus was staring intently. He was still frowning.

'I don't know . . .' He handed the glasses suddenly to Paul. 'We'll go across to him,' he said. 'You watch him and don't take your eyes off him. You can see him, can't you—without the binoculars?'

'Yes,' said Paul, feeling cold. 'Just.'

Gus was already on the winch, winding in the slack. 'He put an arm up and waved. He never has before.'

'But even if it's gone wrong, he can swim all right,' Paul said.

Gus didn't mention the possibility that was in his mind. 'I'll go and start the engine. The chain's ready to break out. But don't you do anything but watch Chris. Don't take your eyes off him.'

Gus's studied efficiency worried Paul more. Chris was just a darker blur on the water in his vision; Paul put his glasses on, but still could not make out what was happening, and dare not look through the binoculars again, in case, in the transition, he lost the blur. But he had thought, when he had seen it magnified, that the figure was on its face. Gus thinks there is something wrong, Paul thought, staring and seeing nothing but the meaningless dark blur. He heard the engine splutter and found himself praying: 'Please, God, let it behave. Make it start.' It started and stopped again. Gus swung it again and its hesitancy agonized Paul. 'God, it must start!' Then the heavy thump broke through the wheezing noises and the smack's bows moved up on the anchor, and Paul tried to make himself relax, staring and saying to himself, 'It's all right, you fool.' He was trembling like a leaf.

'You've still got him?' Gus asked, rattling in the anchor as the old smack forged slowly ahead.

'Yes.'

'Good.' Gus took a few quick turns of the chain round the winch and, leaving the anchor hanging against the stem, sprinted back aft and opened the throttle. Paul heard the hiss of water springing up round the bows and felt the vibrations of the old timbers running up his spine. He felt better now that they were moving, but the fear in his throat was something he had never experienced before. Gus came up beside him and picked up the binoculars.

'What's he doing?' he muttered. 'I can't make it out. He looks as if he's waving his legs in the air.'

'Is he swimming?' Paul asked.

'No.'

'Is he—is——' Paul's voice wouldn't work properly. He cleared his throat and said, 'What shall we do?'

'See what's up first. You go on watching him, to be on the safe side. I'll get a warp out. It might be nothing.'

He went back to the tiller to adjust *Swannie*'s course and then Paul heard him thumping about below, finding a warp. What did he want a warp for? To heave Chris on board? Paul could feel his knees shaking with pure funk inside his cold jeans. He felt inadequate to the point of imbecility, the fear paralysing all his sense. He stared, and could make nothing of the dark spot on the water save that it existed, and drifted with the tide. *Swansong* closed the distance gradually, the old engine thumping noisily.

Gus came back for the binoculars and had another look. He didn't say anything, frowning, and Paul waited, not able to look at his expression for looking at Chris, and almost weeping at the inadequacy of his eyesight.

Then, rather slowly, Gus said, 'He seems submerged, save for his legs. I can't make it out. It doesn't look too good, Paul.' For the first time there was anxiety in his voice, and he looked at Paul uncertainly, momentarily showing the same fear that had Paul pinched and white as paper, crouching on the hatch. Gus knew that whatever had to be done, it was for him to decide. There were no other boats to be seen, save for a white yacht well out beyond the Bench Head. Both shores were over a mile distant.

'Keep on watching him,' he said. 'And if he disappears go on watching the spot.'

The words made Paul feel physically sick. *Swannie* was already at full throttle, and the distance now seemed to be closing fast. Gus had finished being scared, having accepted the worst, and was working out a plan of action. He stood at the tiller, his eyes screwed up with concentration. When they were quite close, and Chris could be seen drifting on the rapid tide, head down and quite stiff, Gus called Paul back aft. He bellowed at him above the racket of the engine, and he came staggering. Tears streamed down his cheeks, but whether they were tears of emotion or the strain of staring, Gus could not tell.

'You've got to take *Swannie*,' Gus said. 'You know how to work the throttle. I'll go close and put her out of gear, so she should stay in the right place.'

Paul nodded.

'I'll try to get the warp round him,' Gus told him. 'We're going to have a hell of a job getting him on board. I'm not going to use the dinghy. It's too cranky.'

He inched the tiller over and eased the throttle lever back. *Swannie* slackened against the flood and her bows slipped towards Chris. Gus looked at Paul.

'You take her now. And for God's sake try to keep by him. I think I'll have to go over, too.'

Paul put a rigid hand on the tiller. He was wondering how he could move the sensitive throttle with his shaking fingers, petrified of doing the wrong thing. He dared not look at Chris any longer. Gus was throwing off his jacket and jersey and kicking off his boots. One end of the warp he had found was made fast on board. It was a very long one. He picked up the free end and climbed outside the shrouds.

'Try to see it doesn't get round the prop,' he shouted. He looked down at the water, hanging out with one hand on the shrouds. *Swannie* was barely making way and Paul couldn't see Chris.

'Are we there?' he almost screamed.

'As you are!' Gus shouted.

The warp in one hand, he slipped down over the bulwarks and Paul saw the coil of rope on deck flake out suddenly as if with a life of its own. Crouched over the gear lever, Paul couldn't see what was going on. The engine was ticking over with a slow, hesitant beat that brought the sweat rolling in beads down Paul's nose. He couldn't see for tears, and was almost paralysed by a feeling of complete unreality, as if the whole thing just wasn't happening. A part of him, cool and detached, was watching the imbecile that was sobbing and muttering over the gear lever, disclaiming all part of the proceedings.

The engine did not cut out, and Paul risked straightening up for a moment.

'Paul!'

Gus was right beside him, one hand clinging to the counter, a scared face upturned.

'Cut the engine out! He—he might go on the screw. Then—take in the warp——'

Paul pressed the button to stop the engine and there was a sudden frightening silence.

'Have you got him?' Paul forced himself to look over the side, clenching his hands. The sickness was cold in his stomach. Chris was still submerged, head down in the water. All Paul could see was the seal-like back with the water washing over it. Gus had tied the rope round Chris's middle and was shaking the bight at Paul.

'Haul it in and make it fast! Then pass me the mainsheet. We'll get two lines on him to make sure, then see if we can heave him clear. The ruddy suit's full of water, save the legs. Hurry up.'

'It *is* true,' Paul thought, as he wound the rope feverishly round a cleat. He scrabbled at the coil of the mainsheet, tangling it hopelessly. 'Chris is drowned.'

'Oh, chuck it down,' Gus growled. 'Just to get it round him.'

Paul watched Gus's strong, bony hands tying knots with fantastic haste and efficiency. Then Gus pulled himself round Chris and clutched the bulwarks.

'Give me a hand.'

Somehow he hauled himself on deck. Paul was tangled in coils of rope, hopelessly trying to help. Gus leaned over and caught the rope round Chris's body and pulled him close, as high as he could.

'Take it up on the cleat!' he muttered. The meaning of the word 'dead-weight' came to him; he only just stopped himself from using it. Paul drew in the slack and made fast, and Gus grabbed for Chris's neck and pulled his head up out of the water.

'We must—get him higher than this,' he grunted. 'Here—help me.'

Paul got down and leaned outboard beside Gus. He got a hand under Chris's jaw and pulled his head up, taking the weight from Gus. The effort was agonizing, dragging his stomach hard down over the bulwarks. Chris's head was as inanimate as a mooring-buoy.

'Got him?'

Paul grunted. Gus moved out from beside him. 'You hold him while I get the jib halyard. We'll get him up on the block. It's the only way.'

The weight dragged Paul down so that he thought he was going overboard. There seemed to be no buoyancy in Chris at all. To hold his face clear of the surface took every ounce of Paul's strength. The warp that held him was as tight as they could get it, but merely held his back a few inches higher than before. His arms half hung, half floated, the mittens pulled back so that the fingers showed starlike and outspread under the dark surface. His face was expressionless, the eyes closed, the skin very pale. A piece of seaweed had looped itself round his neck and streamed in the tide like green ribbon.

'All right?' Paul heard Gus say behind him. There was the shirring noise of a halyard running through a block and the squelch of Gus's wet clothes. 'I'm being as quick as I can. Here.' Gus bent down beside him and Paul got a glimpse of a shackle in his hand. He attached it to the rope round Chris.

'Steady him while I heave away. It might lift his head clear, at least.'

With the purchase on the block to lend weight to the pull, Gus stood at the mast and bore down on the halyard that was now shackled to Chris. Paul felt the weight ease on his own chest, and stinging cramps shot up his arms. Chris's shoulders came out of the water and when Paul relaxed his hold, the limp head hung clear. The arms dangled, splayed out.

'Come and give me a hand now,' Gus said. 'It's going to take all our beef.'

Gus counted, and they hauled down together until their feet swung off the deck. Every few inches of rope gained was cleated down feverishly until Chris's shoulders were up on a level with the top of the bulwarks.

'I think we'll get him now,' Gus said, and they went to Chris and picked him up and lifted him on to the bulwarks. Gus banged him on the back while he was still head down, to get the water out of his lungs, then lowered away on the halyard until he lay on the deck. Gus undid the rope and Paul pulled the suit away from round Chris's neck, tearing open the zippers. Chris did not stir.

'Oh, God,' Gus said softly. 'What do we do now?'

He dared not look at Paul. He wiped his nose on the back of his hand and looked out over the water. The yacht they had seen out by the Bench Head was reaching past them some thirty yards off and Gus saw the man at the tiller staring at them. Gus stood up, waving violently, and shouted across the water:

'Ahoy! We want some help!'

'It's too late,' Paul said.

'No, it isn't. There's that kiss of life thing, or artificial respiration. He'll come round,' Gus said roughly. 'Look, this bloke's coming to help. He'll know something.'

Paul had done artificial respiration when he had been a Wolf-

Cub. Practice on a giggling child was not the same as being faced with one's drowned brother. Chris lay on his face, his head turned to one side. Paul knelt beside him and put his hands on either side of Chris's ribs and swung tentatively forward. He did not feel trembling and half-demented any more, but numb. He heard Gus talking and the rattle of an anchor chain, some thumps along *Swannie*'s side, but did not look up. He swung all his weight on to the hands on Chris's sides, but did not know how long to stay down. There had been counting when he had done it in the Cubs; he could not remember it. He could not remember anything. He could feel the tears running down his cheeks, but he did not feel as if he was crying, just as if he had no feelings at all.

'Here. Let me take over.'

A hand descended on his shoulder and moved him firmly out of the way.

'I don't think it's any good,' Paul said.

'Rubbish,' the man said. His hands were twice the size of Paul's, and his weight, swinging down on either side of Chris's ribs, markedly compressed the limp body on the deck. He hung over, leaning down on Chris, for a few seconds, then sank back on his heels, his hands relaxing. Then again.

'We'll want something warm,' he said briefly. 'Blankets. Put the kettle on.'

Paul stood up. He looked at Gus over the man's head. He could not believe that Chris would ever want blankets or a cup of tea again, but there was a look on Gus's face that stirred a faint hope.

'Go and put the kettle on,' Gus said.

Paul went below, aware that Gus wanted him occupied. The man had said 'Rubbish' just to please him. He filled the kettle, but could not find any matches. He concentrated on looking for the matches in all the likely places, making himself think about matches. His hands were shaking again. Paul despised himself. The matches were in the locker with the cups. If he started to let himself think that Chris was dead, he knew he would go out of control. He crouched over the primus and lit the match.

The hatch darkened and Gus came down. He was blue and his teeth were chattering.

'Have we got any dry clothes on board?' he asked.

'Only Chris's.'

'He'll want those in a minute.'

'You can have my jersey,' Paul said. 'I've got a shirt and vest.'

'Mr. Winnington might have some on board. I'll ask him. He's been away a few days, so he should have.'

'Is that Mr. Winnington? *Woodwind*, you mean?'

'Yes. Didn't you recognize him?'

'No.'

The conversation was ridiculously sane. Paul began to think it was all a bad dream. He left the kettle on the roaring primus and went back on deck and knelt down by Chris, out of Mr. Winnington's way. He put the palms of his hands together, and knew why people wrung their hands in despair; he only stopped doing it because the cliché phrase came to him and it seemed stupid. 'Why do I keep thinking such stupid thoughts?' he wondered. Winnington said nothing, and Paul could see that he was counting to himself as he swung—very slowly, it seemed to Paul—forward and back. Paul looked at him closely. He looked in his late twenties. He had a very firm and handsome face like someone on the television, Paul thought, with very curly brown hair, and an air of great confidence. Paul hoped he was as confident as he looked. His yacht lay alongside, both boats lying to her anchor. Paul could see Birdsmarsh a mile away, unaware of what was happening. The water was grey and calm, as it had been earlier.

Chris had not moved. His lips were slightly open, bluish in colour, and his features seemed to have taken on a fragile, porcelain look. Paul could see the tiny scar on his cheek-bone where he had got hung up in the barbed wire when Herbert, the old bull, had chased him several years ago. Paul tried to remember how long one did artificial respiration for before deciding it was no good. But he didn't know. He glanced at his watch. Mr. Winnington had been doing it for nearly ten minutes. He remembered that Chris had wanted to meet Mr. Winnington.

'How's things?' Gus said gruffly, coming to squat beside him. He had changed into dry clothes. 'Shouldn't be long now.'

Paul said nothing. He was cold as ice and his limbs were shaking helplessly. He stared at Chris's marble face and the limp, half-clenched fingers, and saw a slight spasm contract the hand. His heart gave a lurch.

'He——' The words stuck in his throat.

'What? Any signs?' Mr. Winnington said sharply.

'I didn't see anything,' Gus said.

Paul shook his head. He did not dare to speak. Mr. Winnington had not paused in his job, but he looked less confident now, and his face was beginning to shine with sweat.

Paul stared at Chris's face, willing it to come to life. He knew what he had seen had been a figment of his stupid imagination. But Gus put out a hand to see if he could feel any breath and Chris quite definitely sighed. Neither Paul nor Gus dared say a word. They looked at Chris, holding their own breath so as not to miss the whisper of his. Paul felt that his self-control was held by threads of gossamer.

'I think——' Mr. Winnington paused, and Chris gave a gasp like a new-born baby. His features contorted suddenly and he moaned. His fingers stiffened. Paul gasped, and felt the hysterical joy mounting inside him like an explosion.

'Chris!'

'Oh, it's worked!' Gus muttered stupidly, feeling suddenly as if he were going to pass out.

'There's some brandy on board *Woodwind*,' Mr. Winnington said sharply. 'In the galley. You'd better get it.'

'I'll go,' Gus said.

'I think we'll all need some,' Winnington said, looking at Paul. He carried on with his task, gently, and Paul watched the feeble stirring of life transform Chris's terrible immobility, convinced that a miracle was taking place before his eyes. It was beyond his comprehension, the mystery of mere living; he felt that the last hour had gone on for days. He suddenly felt very sick, and had to get up and scramble across to the bulwarks, just as if they were out in a North Sea gale.

By the time Chris was breathing on his own and showing signs of returning consciousness, Gus had produced a large bottle of brandy, Paul had made a strong brew of tea, and Mr. Winnington himself was lighting what he considered a well-earned cigarette. Chris was stripped of his suit and wet clothes and bundled in blankets.

'As soon as we can we'll move him on to *Woodwind*. I'll light the stove and get a fug up,' Mr. Winnington said.

'I'll do it,' Gus said, happy to move about the handsome yacht as if she was his own.

Mr. Winnington was surveying Chris's exposure suit curiously, but he said nothing. He looked at Paul and said, 'Are you the Fairfax boys?'

Paul nodded.

'I thought I knew your faces.' He glanced down at Chris, thoughtfully, and drew on his cigarette. 'I'll try to get a drop of brandy down him in a minute,' he said, after a pause. 'He's almost round.'

It was some time before Chris realized what had happened, and well into the afternoon before he was able to sit up in *Woodwind*'s bunk and gingerly put his feet on the floor.

'Some fishing-party you're going to have to explain away,' Gus said to Paul, looking at Chris's pale face.

'We've got to get ashore, as a point of interest,' Mr. Winnington said. 'He's a hospital case, rightly.'

'Oh, no, I'm not,' Chris said quickly.

Woodwind and *Swannie*, too late to catch the flood into the harbour, lay at anchor outside to await the next tide. *Swannie*'s crew had repaired to the comfort of *Woodwind*'s cabin, where they now sat, drinking tea.

'You don't just get up and walk away from a little episode like that,' Peter Winnington said to Chris.

'No, but not hospital,' Chris said.

'He doesn't want anyone to know what he was doing,' Gus explained. 'He was experimenting.'

'The experiment, I presume, was unsuccessful,' Winnington said dryly. 'Just what was that suit you were wearing?'

Gus explained, to save Chris the effort. Chris had blue shadows under his eyes, and had said very little the whole afternoon. Paul was also silent, almost as pale as Chris, but Gus, gratified by the knowledge that he had risen to the crisis with a cool efficiency that he had never known before that he possessed, was full of spirits. It was pure pleasure now, to be sitting in the shining saloon of the admired *Woodwind*, talking to the elusive Mr. Winnington, even wearing the dapper Mr. Winnington's shoregoing trousers and white pullover.

'What went wrong this morning, then?' Winnington asked. He offered his cigarettes round and Chris and Gus both took one. Chris leaned forward to the match Gus held out.

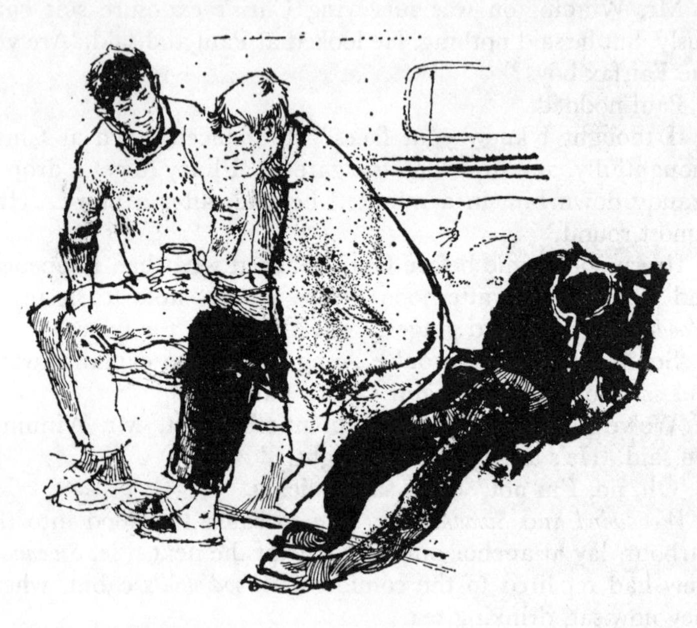

'I hit a dirty great lump of timber, all splinters. I couldn't get out of the way in time, and with that tide running and the lop on the water, it was quite an impact. It ripped a hole in the back and when I turned over, the chest compartment must have got it, too, because the next thing I knew the only buoyancy I had was in the legs. I managed to keep up for a bit, but I knew it was a losing battle.'

Chris pulled on the cigarette, hoping it would get rid of the awful taste in his mouth. He did not want to think about what had gone wrong. He just wanted to weather the terrible weakness that possessed him and start again on his suit without anyone making a fuss. What had happened made no difference to his faith in it, only he knew other people would shake their heads, which made it all the more important to get on with proving it again. Stabbing, vomiting pains wracked his diaphragm. He stubbed out the cigarette.

'If we can get you ashore, I can drive you home,' Winnington said.

'I can't go home like this,' Chris said involuntarily.

Anything that stood in his way was merely milking off the energy he wanted to spend on his suit. The purpose of keeping the whole thing from his parents was only to avoid tiresomeness: now, particularly, they must not know what had happened. He would not stop what he was doing whatever they said, but he was too good-natured to want to have any fuss. His mother was sensible, but she wouldn't understand that it was all perfectly straightforward. Nothing would convince her that it wasn't risky. But he wouldn't be able to hide from her now what he felt like.

Winnington frowned. 'You can stay on board. I don't mind. But I don't like being responsible for you, without a doctor seeing you.'

'Surely it's only a matter of resting now. I'll be as right as rain in a few hours,' Chris said.

'Well, it's up to you. I dare say getting you ashore would be pretty exhausting, at least until high water. That's not until the small hours now, is it? One o'clock, roughly. If you like, you can rest here till then, then you can come home with me and sleep it off at my place. Go home in the morning.'

Chris nodded gratefully.

'Someone'll have to make an appearance at home,' Paul protested.

'That's you,' Gus said, grinning.

'You can say Chris met me and I'm entertaining him aboard for the evening,' Mr. Winnington said with a slight smile. 'Perfectly true. If he looks a bit under the weather in the morning, they will think he's got a hangover.'

Paul groaned softly. 'Are you coming?' he said to Gus.

Gus glanced at *Woodwind*'s owner. 'Mr. Winnington might need some help at high water,' he said. 'If Chris is groggy . . .'

Paul looked at Gus, disgusted. 'What about *your* parents, then? Won't they be wondering what's become of *you*?'

'That'll be the day, when they worry,' Gus said briefly.

Paul had forgotten. The parent-burden was all his.

'I'll help you slide the dinghy over the mud,' Gus said.

Paul looked at Chris. 'You're—you're all right, then?' He was still seeing Chris's face as it had been, bluish-white like best china, and the hair hanging in locks like damp, dead leaves. He didn't feel he would ever lose the image, and that, through him, his mother was bound to see it, too, whatever he said about Chris being with Mr. Winnington.

'Yes,' Chris said.

'All right. I'll go.'

Gus put on his gum boots and rowed Paul in the dinghy to the edge of the mud, where they both got out over the stern. Leaning their weight on the small dinghy, they pushed it before them over the mud, struggling to free each foot as it sank deep behind them. Without the dinghy for support the journey would have been impossible. When they got to the saltings Gus stopped and Paul scrambled gratefully up on to the spongy sea-lavender roots. He turned round and Gus grinned up at him.

'Quite a day, eh?'

'I don't want another like it in a hurry,' Paul said.

'If you go into the village, you can tell my mother I'll be home at high water. If you feel like it. It's not important, though.'

'All right.'

On his own, Paul walked slowly along the sea-wall towards the village. He felt very tired, weighed down by the thought that if Chris had depended on him for his life, he would indeed have been dead. Gus had saved Chris's life, Gus and Mr. Winnington. Paul felt an overwhelming shame at his own feelings of blind panic during the rescue. He remembered clawing at the mainsheet and throwing it to Gus in a tangled mess, gasping with panic over the throttle, while Gus, who had never been known to put a foot in the river except in the height of a heat-wave, had cold-bloodedly gone overboard.

'I was a disgusting coward,' Paul thought, and self-contempt blotted out any feelings of thankfulness at the outcome of the incident. Now it seemed that the whole thing had happened merely to reveal the shortcomings in his character. It wasn't that he had any great opinion of himself, anyway, especially since his father had been pitching into him about his attitude to the marina business, but he hadn't ever discovered before just what a hysterical ass he was. Snivelling like a girl and being sick over *Woodwind's* shining topsides. Not that he cared about being a hero, just to have some self-respect. He walked doggedly along the churned-up track, cold and dispirited. He tried to think that if Chris had been drowned he would really have had something to be miserable about, but now that the stark threat was past it no longer seemed to have any impact. Things nearly happen, Paul thought, often. But they don't quite. Not to oneself, only to other people. But one day, logic told him, he might be one of the other people.

Gus's mother came to the door and took Paul's message sourly.

'Well, I hope he's not expecting me to wait up for him, that's all,' she said. 'Bloomin' lodger, that boy. The sooner he gets out to work and stops wasting his time the better.'

Paul wanted to tell her that Gus was brave and worth six of her, but merely turned away and set off for his own home. He, who was stupid and panicky as a hen, would get a kind welcome and a dinner waiting. It didn't make sense.

6

THE MAN IN THE MOONLIGHT

Chris came home at twelve o'clock the next morning. Paul was in the kitchen, mooning around restlessly and getting in his mother's way. She had twice asked him if he felt all right, but as Mr. Glass had come down with an architect and was at that moment pacing the sea-wall, she put his moodiness down to the visitors.

'He's a bit ahead of himself, isn't he?' Paul said. 'He hasn't got planning permission yet, has he?'

'No. But I imagine he will, so don't hold out hopes, Paul. You're making it very hard for yourself.'

'Oh, I don't care any more,' Paul lied crossly. 'I just hope he falls in and drowns himself, that's all.'

Drowning was still uppermost in his mind. His mother was rolling out pastry and Paul was thinking, 'This time yesterday Chris was drowning. What if she knew?'

When Chris came in all she said was, 'Had a good time? There's some tea in the pot if you want a cup.'

'Oh, thanks. Yes.'

Chris looked normal enough, to Paul's relief, only weary. He poured himself a cup of tea and sat down in the big Windsor chair with arms.

'I won't offer you a biscuit, because lunch won't be long. We've got our Mayfair speculator down today,' Mrs. Fairfax said.

'He's not staying to lunch?' Paul said.

'Yes, of course. And a little civility from you, please, whatever you think about his job. I didn't know you were a friend of Mr. Winnington's, Chris.'

'Well, only since yesterday,' Chris said.

Paul stood at the table, rolling a little sausage of pastry in his hands. Mothers were so nosy, he was thinking, even the best of them. What if she really knew how Chris and Mr. Winnington met? The deceit they were practising made him feel cross and uncomfortable. But Chris was a man now, he told himself. He could do as he pleased.

The evasion did not worry him as it had worried Paul. There was no secrecy in his face, only, under his eyes, the shadows of his being drowned, which his mother might notice, but not read correctly. Paul relaxed slightly, and tried to put himself into a better humour.

'He's quite an interesting bloke, Winnington,' Chris said. 'What does he do for a living?'

'He works in Chelmsford, I believe, something to do with electronics. Experimental stuff. I don't know much about him, only village gossip.' Mrs Fairfax said.

'That means you know everything about him,' Paul said.

His mother smiled. 'I'm sure I don't know why he lives so far from his work, in a remote spot like this. Did you go to his place, then, Chris?'

'Yes. He lives with an older bloke called Warner, up at the Research Station.'

'But the Research Station is oysters and things, isn't it?' Paul said. 'Why does he live there?'

'Because Warner is a relative of his,' Chris said. 'I can't remember what. Uncle, perhaps. They seem to have a lot in common. Warner runs the fishery research place, but he struck me as being a very knowledgeable man—apart from his job, I mean. So did Peter, come to that.'

'Peter is Winnington?' asked Paul.

'Yes. He was at Cambridge, too.'

Chris was bound to like Winnington, Paul thought, knowing that he had saved his life. In the same way that one felt a glow of affection for the dentist when he cleared up one's misery with a few minutes' work. Only more so.

'Your washing's all ready to pack, Chris,' Mrs. Fairfax said, indicating a pile of neat linen on the dresser. 'Have you looked up a train yet?'

'No, not yet.'

'Why, when are you going back?' Paul asked.

'Tomorrow.'

'What, as soon as that? I thought you had weeks yet.'

'No. Tomorrow.'

Mrs. Fairfax went out to talk to the grocer, who thumped on the back door at this opportune moment, and Paul said to Chris, 'Honestly, will you be all right? I'd forgotten you had to go back——'

'Yes, but listen. I'm in a bit of a fix.' Chris spoke urgently, in a low voice. 'I've got to take the suit back with me—or what remains of it. And it's still on *Swannie*. Do you think you can go and collect it for me?'

'Yes, of course. I'll go at high water.'

Chris glanced at the clock. 'That's in an hour.'

'I'll go now, then.'

Chris looked relieved. 'Splendid. I was getting worried.'

Paul went out to the porch and put his gum boots on.

'Hey, where do you think you're going?' his mother said. 'Lunch is nearly ready.'

'Oh, I won't be half an hour,' Paul said.

'No, you won't. Because you're staying here, my lad. I know your half-hours. You said you'd be back for lunch yesterday, if you remember.'

'Oh, Mum——'

Paul's heart sank. His mother was already laying the table. It was special today, too, with a cloth and the best glasses, and he remembered the speculator and the architect. There would be talk and slow, thin carving, and no getting down until they were all finished. He looked at Chris, and Chris shrugged. They knew they were beaten.

Mr. Glass came in with his friend and Mr. Fairfax an hour later. Paul knew he could have been down to the harbour and back by the time they sat down to table, but his mother showed no remorse for her unnecessary stricture. Paul mumbled at Mr. Glass and the architect, Mr. Butler, when his father made the introductions, but Chris made easy, interested conversation, as if he had no troubles, no mangled invention to rescue. Even if he didn't hate Mr. Glass, Paul thought, he couldn't be charming like Chris. He would never be charming and confident, not if he lived to be a hundred. He watched Mr. Glass mopping up roast lamb, laughing, chatting away about sluices and access roads; he watched his gold filling sparkling under his full, jolly lips, the exaggerated arch of his big nostrils, the fat, well-fed jowls of his wide, blue jaw. He noted the nylon shirt and gold cuff-links, and the thin black hair over the shining dome of the sharp business brain. He wore a diamond ring. Paul hated everything he saw so much that he could scarcely eat, let alone talk. He could visualize Mr. Glass at his usual lunch in a big London place, laying fivers on the plate to pay the bill, and the fivers all extorted from innocent pastures where cows grazed and the skylarks went up from under your feet at every step.

'How could you speak to him?' he said to Chris when they had gone. It was three o'clock, and the tide was lost.

'He's all right,' Chris said. 'It's only his job, after all.'

'I reckon he thought our young 'un was an idiot,' Mr. Fairfax said. 'You'd better get outside and see to Lily, Paul. I think she's starting her calf. I've got to go into Maldon this afternoon, so just you keep an eye on her, and if I'm not back, start the milking.'

'All right.'

Paul was glad to get back to where he belonged, away from the pressures of things that he could not manage. The smell of the cowshed was clean after Mr. Glass's Country Talcum. He forgot about Chris, and spent the afternoon with Lily, who did not know what was happening to her and was quiet when Paul was there. His father did not come back and he did the milking and went back to Lily and delivered a bull-calf at six o'clock. By the time he had cleaned up he felt pleasantly tired and soothed, and Mr. Glass's Jaguar had gone. He had forgotten all about Chris's suit, until he went indoors.

'Oh, cripes! Chris! That damned thing!'

'I was going to go myself,' Chris said, 'but it wouldn't be any good. I just couldn't, the way I feel at the moment.'

Paul glanced at the clock. 'It'll be high water again before long. I'll go tonight, about two. It'll be a lot easier.'

Chris raised his eyebrows. 'What about——'

'Oh, it's easy enough,' Paul said. 'I've often gone out at night, if there's a moon and there's some waders or something I want to watch. Mum never hears a thing. I go down the pantry roof, out of the spare-room window.'

Chris looked surprised, but did not argue.

The sea-wall was different by night. A half-moon, sharp with frost, flooded the colourless, empty fields, and spiked the full ditches with reflected light. Paul walked down the hard track, trying to hold back from getting emotional about Mr. Glass's plans, trying not to think of access roads and concrete promenades. A weasel slipped across his track. 'It doesn't matter,' Paul kept saying. He came up the sea-wall and the river was bright with reflected stars like a summer field with daisies. He looked at it coldly, but the soft night-call of a restless curlew dissolved his unconcern; it warbled with a poignancy that made his heart turn over in his chest. 'It doesn't matter,' he said out loud, and the curlew answered him with a mocking repeat that Paul thought must be the voice of all the little, doomed things in the world. Its ringing sadness was his own, as if the curlew were singing his own true feelings into the darkness, while he stood there muttering like a dummy, 'It doesn't matter.'

'God,' he thought, 'no wonder they think I'm cracked.'

He was conscious of a desolation over and beyond the curlew's song that was too awful to contemplate. He turned back from it, bringing himself to reality by saying some swear words and stamping away along the track to the harbour.

'What a nit,' he thought to himself, 'what a girl I am. Crikey, how right they all are! As if anything matters that much . . . the damned curlew—it's worse than Beethoven, getting you all het up . . .'

He pulled his mind on to the matter in hand, afraid of how he could feel if he let himself go. He decided he wouldn't let it show any more, what he felt. At home, he would act dead-pan, and they could think what they pleased.

'Play it cool, boy,' he said to himself, and the curlew's call hovered over the sea-wall, shredded by a thin breeze. Paul could feel the sea breathing in the saltings, and the stars in the water splintered and scattered in cat's-paws of wind. 'Oh, God,' he prayed, 'please don't make it matter so much.'

It was high water when he got to the harbour and he could see *Swannie* lying in the deep channel just behind *Woodwind*. A man in a dinghy was rowing towards the hard. The wake splayed out behind him in a silver V, scarcely broken by the breeze, and seemed to come straight off *Swannie*'s stern.

Paul, surprised to see anyone else abroad at this time of night, walked on towards the hard, trying to make out if the figure was Gus. But the man rowed too quickly for Gus. He went alongside the top of the hard, climbed out with the painter and made it fast to one of the ring-bolts. Then he went back and secured the oars, turned away over the sea-wall and disappeared. Shortly afterwards, while Paul was still some fifty yards away, the sound of a powerful car engine broke the silence. Paul couldn't see the car, because it was hidden by some old motor boats that lay on the side of the road, but it sounded to him like Mr. Winnington's Aston Martin. By the time he reached the hard the car had gone.

'How odd,' Paul said, out loud.

He went down to the dinghy, which was *Swannie*'s, untied the painter and got in. The oars were still dripping when he lifted them up. He pushed off and started to row clumsily towards the smack. He was sure that the man he had seen was Peter Winnington, and he was trying to think what he had been doing. His first reaction was that what he had seen was very odd, but as he rowed he conceded that the dead of night made any quite normal action full of sinister overtones.

'He probably went to look at *Woodwind*, and used our dinghy because it was handy,' he thought.

The tide carried the dinghy past *Woodwind* and down on to *Swannie*. Paul attempted a neat back-paddle to go alongside, and hit *Swannie*'s counter with a crash that almost threw him off the thwart. He dropped the oars and grabbed for her bulwarks, but the dinghy had already moved off on the tide and he was obliged to scramble for the oars and turn round to plug back against the current. Gus always went alongside as sweetly as if *Swannie* were made of glass. Paul was ashamed of himself and glad that there was no one to see his clown performance. When at last he hauled himself out on deck he discovered that he didn't even know a knot to make the dinghy fast with. Gus's nonchalant bowline was beyond him.

'This sailing,' he muttered, fumbling over the painter. 'It's all tricks and jargon.'

Aloof in the moonlight, *Swannie*, he felt, disowned him. She wasn't his hide-out any more. He stumbled down the hatchway and groped round for Chris's suitcase. It was on the bunk, and the suit was neatly folded inside it. The cabin smelt of cigarette smoke.

'How odd,' Paul thought again.

It wasn't his imagination, because he hadn't been looking for clues. The smell was just there, unmistakable. Winnington smoked, Paul thought. But why . . .?

'Oh, so what,' Paul said to himself, and hauled the suitcase up on deck. He realized suddenly that he felt very tired, and he was glad his mission was nearly completed. He rowed back to the hard and set off for home with the suitcase, his eyes on the hard mud ruts under his feet, his mind a blank.

'Why,' Paul thought, 'does Chris have to go on with this thing? Why does he have to get me involved? I've got enough worries of my own.'

He lay on the sea-wall, looking down on *Swannie*, back in her old mud-berth. Spring had got under way at last, and the sun was warming scents out of the earth that Paul had forgotten were there. A letter from Chris was in his hand.

'The damage isn't very bad,' Chris wrote. 'With a few refinements to complete, we reckon we shall be ready to give the suit its serious testing in two or three months' time. Peter agreed to help me with this, using his yacht, so if you see him around, perhaps you could tell him the good news. When I know it's ready for sure I will get in touch with him.'

Paul didn't want to be an accomplice to this test. He didn't want to tell Peter Winnington the good news; he didn't even like Peter Winnington, he had decided. He was too cocky and too smooth, and had a derisive way of looking at you, Paul thought.

'Hi, I've got news for you.' Gus came down the wall, slithering on his heels. He was wearing tight crumpled jeans and a black leather jacket. It was Saturday and he had been for an interview with his prospective employer.

'How did you get on?' Paul asked.

'Oh, it's not that.' Gus grimaced. He dismissed his interview with a few brief rude words. 'I met Sydney just now, that's the thing. He was telling me that there's going to be a race for gaff-rigged boats on the Blackwater in August, and why don't we enter *Swannie*. Well, why not? What do you think?'

'A race?' Paul wasn't very interested. 'If you like,' he added, remembering that he was the owner of the boat.

'You mean it?' Gus looked anxious. 'I mean, I'm dead keen, so if you're game I'll try to get her fit. There'll be a lot to do between now and then.'

'All right. I don't mind.'

'Don't get blood pressure or anything—with excitement, I mean,' Gus said sarcastically.

Paul was not amused. 'What am I supposed to do, then? Get up and dance?'

Gus groaned. 'Oh, no, but you don't have to be such a ruddy wet. I don't know what's wrong with you these days. You don't deserve to have a boat like that, the interest you take.'

'I didn't *buy* her, did I? I was quite happy when she was just a place to come to. I'd give fifty of her for Mr. Glass to be run over by a bus.'

'Oh, then Sydney's up to something else that'll probably interest you more. He's organizing an objectors' meeting, or something, to your Mr. Glass's plans. Got speakers coming from London, and naturalist blokes and what not. Stirring it all up. To crystallize local opinion, he said. Whatever that might mean.'

'Oh, good for old Syd! Now that *is* news.'

'It won't do any good,' Gus said. 'It's just peanuts against someone like Glass.'

'Well, it's better than nothing. You never know.'

'Huh.' Gus looked sour. His eyes went to *Swannie* and the frown went out of his face. 'She's fast, you know, Paul. What if we won, eh?'

'Yes, what?' Paul muttered. He had decided he didn't like Gus much either sometimes. Sometimes he couldn't think of anyone he liked much at all. He handed Chris's letter to Gus. 'Look.'

Gus read it. 'Old Winnington'd probably want some crew for a trip like that,' he said.

'You talk to him about it, then.'

'All right, I will.'

'Really? And tell me what he says? Then I won't have to bother. Chris is bound to want it all promised.'

'Yes, all right.'

'I don't like Winnington.'

'Oh, for heaven's sake, what's *he* done?'

'Well, poking around on *Swannie*, for one thing.' It was the only tangible thing Paul could think up. Gus, who had already offered up several plausible reasons for this midnight expedition, looked at Paul impatiently.

'You don't even know if it was him, for a start,' he said. 'And if you think it's so funny, why don't you ask him about it, instead of cooking up a great mystery? No doubt he'd have a perfectly simple explanation.'

'You ask him, then. When you talk to him about Chris's suit. Ask him what he went back to *Swannie* for.'

'All right, I will,' Gus said rashly.

'And tell me what he says.'

'All right, you old woman.' Gus got up and stood looking at

Swannie. His long thick hair blew across his forehead in the warm breeze. Paul glanced up at him and thought suddenly that he no more looked like a schoolboy than Sydney Peacemaker. Gus bore with him, Paul thought, because he owned *Swannie*; there was no other reason. When Gus had gone Paul lay on the bank, feeling lonely and depressed. The sun was a mockery. It was his own sea-wall beneath him, and his own saltings, hazing over with the first buds of the sea thrift, and Gus was too blind to see what mattered. They were all blind, Gus, and Winnington, and even Chris. Paul knew that he was still a child and that Gus had grown up, and he hated Gus for being so capable, and himself for being such a fool.

7
THE OBJECTORS' MEETING

It wasn't that anything moved quickly that summer. There was nothing, Paul thought, that one could do, only go on at school and on the farm with the worries over one's head gathering strength or dispersing, as the case may be, like summer storm-clouds. Apart from Mr. Glass, Paul worried over Chris's coming trial with Mr. Winnington, and when he stopped think-about that Gus would reintroduce the subject of the race. Paul did not want to have anything to do with the race, and still less to be a party to Chris's business. He felt that he was being dragged against his will into other people's things; they expected him to be concerned, but they none of them cared twopence for the only thing that possessed his mind. Chris came home one week-end in order to see Peter Winnington, and Paul went with him to the Research Station and sat on the lawn behind the trim, secluded house and the Fishery Laboratories and listened to their conversation. Gus had asked Winnington what he had been doing on *Swannie* the night Paul went to retrieve the suit, and Winnington had said he had never been near *Swannie* that night.

'He didn't know what on earth I was talking about,' Gus had told Paul.

Sitting with Chris, Paul remembered Gus's scorn. He thought, 'Peter Winnington is a liar,' and watched him carefully as he chatted to Chris. It was difficult, in fact, not to be attracted to Winnington; perversely, it was his over-abundance of attractiveness that put Paul off. And yet there was nothing contrived about it. His extreme good looks were of a rugged, athletic type, not in any way effeminate, and Paul could well believe that he could handle *Woodwind* alone in whatever the North Sea sent, as Gus averred. Now, just home from work, he wore a white shirt with the tie pulled loose and well-creased grey trousers. He sat in a deck-chair with a whisky and soda in his hand, and listened attentively to Chris's plans.

'An exact date will be decided by the tide, I suppose,' Winnington said. 'You say you will be ready by the middle of

July. I've got some days off work due to me, so if we work out what'll suit us best I'll get my time off fixed.'

He went indoors and fetched a tide-table and a tidal chart of the coast, and they pushed their glasses back and conferred over the garden table. Paul watched them. He was trying to remember that night he had seen the dinghy coming away from *Swannie*. The more he thought about it, the less he could remember exactly what the figure had looked like, and what exactly the course of the dinghy had been.

'July the 24th would suit,' Chris said. 'The ebb would take us out at midday and we could start the stint at six, say, far enough off shore for the flood not to carry us back. It's neaps then. And the night-time stretch can be done fairly early on while we're still fresh.'

'Not July the 24th,' Paul said. 'That's the date Sydney's fixed the meeting about Birdsmarsh.'

Chris looked at him impatiently. 'Well, does that matter?'

Paul could hardly form his words. He stared at Chris, his lips twitching with anger. 'You—you—oh, Chris, you——'

'Oh, all right. I suppose it does,' Chris said, not very graciously. He turned back to the tide-table. 'The day after, then. The 25th.'

'Assuming we have a good forecast,' Winnington said. 'You don't want to do it in a gale, do you?'

'Not a gale. But I'm not bothered about a bit of wind, unless it makes it more difficult for you.'

'Well, no. I shall heave-to, and lie comfortably enough. Theoretically we should stay pretty well together. *Woodwind* might forereach slightly, say half a knot, but not enough to make things awkward.'

Paul watched Chris bitterly, feeling almost as if his brother had turned round and hit him. Chris, unaware of Paul's animosity, was checking a chart with the tide-table, working out his probable course. Paul, remembering him as the limp, seal-like object that Gus had rescued, shuddered at the enthusiasm he generated, hating him and yet feeling terribly responsible for his safety, as if he owed it to their parents. Nothing would convince Paul now that Chris's invention was safe, after what had happened, yet Chris's faith was unshaken.

He was like the birdman, Paul thought, who had jumped off the Eiffel Tower. It was clear that the fate of the farm—his home—was as unimportant in his mind as the gnat that was now drowning in his glass of beer. Paul glowered, swinging his legs in the garden chair.

'You want to come on this trip, don't you?' Chris said to him, as if conscious that he had been unkind. 'You'll enjoy it in a yacht like *Woodwind*.'

'Yes, I want to come,' Paul said. The fact that Chris thought he might enjoy it only underlined the disparity in their thinking. *Enjoy* it! He only wanted to go because he couldn't stay at home not knowing what was happening. He felt a morbid compulsion to go, compounded of duty, curiosity, and this dreadful weight of responsibility. It was hardly anticipation of the kind Chris imagined.

When Gus heard the date that had been fixed for the test he looked at Paul in dismay.

'You idiot! I'll have started work by then! Surely you knew that? I start the day after school finishes.'

'Don't blame me! I didn't fix it, did I? Go and complain to Chris.'

'But I wanted to come,' Gus muttered. 'Oh, I wanted to come!' It was almost a wail.

'Oh, look, I'm sorry,' Paul said. 'But honestly, it was nothing to do with me. Surely you can get the day off to do it? Or start a few days later than you said you would? You ought to have a bit of a holiday, anyway. I've never heard of anyone starting a job the minute school ends.'

'Yeah, well, that's Dad's doing, not mine. He reckons I've been on holiday all the time, up till now. And if I take a day off as soon as I'm started—well, it's more than my life's worth.'

'I'd sooner you went than me,' Paul said.

'That doesn't help any,' Gus said.

'Perhaps I could ask Mr. Winnington if you could go with him some time.'

'Yes, but——' Gus hesitated. 'I'm not his type, really. I was going to ask him, but you can't, really. Not just ask someone. It's like asking yourself to dinner or something. Besides, if you notice, he doesn't sail just to amuse himself. Whenever he sails he goes off on a long trip, Holland usually, from what I gather. I get the feeling it's something to do with business, not just holiday trips.'

Paul was surprised. 'Yes, now you come to mention it, I've never seen *Woodwind* just pottering around at week-ends.'

'That's why I thought this trip with Chris would be all right for me. Because I could work my passage. He'll need some help if it's going to last twenty-four hours.'

'I hope he doesn't think *I'm* any good,' Paul said. He felt genuinely sorry for Gus and would have given anything to have him go. Gus spent more and more time on *Swannie* as the time for him to start work drew nearer. If the weather was fine, he went down to *Swannie* instead of to school, and his reputation with the authorities, never of the highest, rapidly deteriorated as his last term drew out. Ratings and canings had proved themselves futile, and he was merely suffered or ignored by frustrated teachers when he condescended to attend.

'It's such a shame to see him behaving like that,' Paul's mother said to her husband after Gus had left the house one Saturday morning with Paul. 'From what I hear about him these days, I'm beginning to wonder whether he's a fit friend for our Paul.' She smiled as she made the remark, to show that she was partly joking.

'Oh, they're all the same, these lads,' Mr. Fairfax said rather crossly. 'Paul's as bad in his way.'

'It's a difficult time for them. And worse for Gus, because his parents are so hopeless. Not that we seem to be able to do much for Paul lately,' she added. 'Sometimes he looks as if he had all the weight of the world on his shoulders.'

'Huh.' Mr. Fairfax disliked the subject of Paul. 'Pity he wasn't a girl.'

Mrs. Fairfax diagnosed this remark as insulting, and said no more on the subject. She smoothed the ironing blanket in front of her and shook out a check shirt. 'Have you decided whether you're going to the meeting on Wednesday?'

'Catch me! If they want my views, they can come and ask for them.'

'I don't think many people in the village object to the business—Paul apart, of course. The ones against seem to be the visitors, like that strange Dr. Peacemaker, and the nature people. And some of the retired people, I believe—Colonel Spiggott and so forth.'

'Blasted cheek, if you ask me. They come here buying up decent working men's cottages at prices no one else in the village can afford, pretty them up with pink paint and roses round the door, then stand up at a public meeting and tell us all what we ought to do. The meeting'll be lousy with 'em, because the ordinary folk who are quite happy about things won't bother to go. They'll be too busy watching the telly.'

'The County Council men are coming. I believe they're going to give Mr. Glass a decision before September. So he said. This meeting is the big chance for the objectors.'

'I've heard that some journalist bloke is coming down to spout,' Mr. Fairfax said. 'One of these old-type huntin', shootin', fishin' brigade. Sort that wants to keep the common people from enjoying themselves. It'll be good for a laugh, Lizzie. I'd go if I didn't think I'd be called upon to defend myself. I'm no good at speechifying.'

'No doubt Paul will tell us all about it, poor kid.'

'Poor kid be damned.'

When Paul set off for the Birdsmarsh Yacht Marina Protest Meeting he almost wished that Chris had kept to his original date and that they were away on *Woodwind*. He felt nervous and awkward, aware that he would be conspicuous at the meeting by reason of his being a Fairfax, but also knowing that he wouldn't have the courage to stand up and say what he thought. In fact, now that it had come to the point, he felt as loath to go as he did to accompany Chris on *Woodwind*. His parents had decided that it would be more tactful if they stayed at home, and Chris was not coming home until late in the evening. Gus had reluctantly promised to go, and Paul called for him on his way to the hall.

'Shan't be a sec,' Gus shouted from the kitchen. 'Make yourself at home.'

Paul stayed propped against the front door, while Gus spent a long time combing his hair, which had become rather long to support his delinquent image, and his mother nagged at him about the dirt he had left round her washing-up bowl. Satisfied at last, he shrugged into his leather jacket and joined Paul at the door. He had been at work three days, and Paul hadn't seen him since the last day at school.

'What's it like at Mason's?' Paul said, as they walked up the street.

'Oh, just as awful as I thought it would be. I've spent three days solid lying on my back chipping filth off the underneaths of ten-ton trucks. When I was stuck under that ruddy lorry this afternoon I remembered all that blah they gave us last week about carrying the torch of learning into the world, and the vicar saying all that stuff about however humble our jobs the right attitude towards our work could make us millionaires of the spirit—you remember?—and I started to laugh. And Reg—that's the boss—came by and said, "What's so ruddy funny under there?" He likes everyone gloomy and yes-sirring all day long. So I said, "Just something I thought of," and he said, "Well, think of six more ruddy ten-tonners to clean off, because that's your ruddy lot between now and Saturday." I bet the ruddy Rev.'s never laid on his back all day chipping filth all over himself.'

Gus kicked a stone out of the gutter and sent it spinning into someone's front garden, narrowly missing an indignant cat. Paul was impressed with Gus's swearing, and supposed that going out to work had liberated his tongue. He had missed Gus the last few days, far more than he had guessed he would, and had an uncomfortable feeling that with Gus starting work life was getting distinctly more earnest. This feeling had closed in on him ever since he heard of Mr. Glass's plan. He could hardly believe that, six months ago, he hadn't a care in the world.

'You going to get up and make a speech?' Gus was asking, as they approached the village hall.

'Can you see me?' Paul growled.

'Don't reckon you'll have to, anyway,' Gus added. 'This is an objectors' meeting, and they'll all be on your side.'

The hall, a rickety structure of corrugated iron that served the Women's Institute, the Parish Council, the clinic, the library, the weekly dancing class, the Darby and Joan Club and the occasional Saturday-night hop, as well as the rare public meetings, was reasonably well filled, with everyone looking round curiously to see which members of the community were taking an interest in the subject. Paul's arrival caused a good deal of nudging, and he took an inconspicuous seat with Gus behind a pillar, wishing he were invisible. Or, better still, brave enough to say in public what he thought of Mr. Glass. When the seats on the platform were taken Paul managed to identify the two representatives of the County Council (modestly dressed in dark suits and well prepared with spectacles and plenty of papers); a solicitor (a fittingly ugly little man with a grey Hitler moustache and sharp, hostile eyes), presumably speaking for Mr. Glass, the chairman of the Parish Council; Dr. Peacemaker; and the man who was obviously the 'well-known writer and broadcaster on country matters'. The last looked like a caricature of a country gentleman, dressed in very hairy tweeds, a check shirt and strong walking-shoes. Paul expected to see a game-dog under his chair. He lived in South Kensington and wrote articles for magazines with titles like 'My Secret Island' and 'Away from it all on the Norfolk Coast'. Paul had never been able to work out why anyone who professed to love these quiet places was so willing to make them known to the public by blazoning them in a newspaper. His heart sank at the thought of his championing the preservation of Birdsmarsh in the *Daily Trumpet*. Facing this assorted platform at the front of the hall was a phalanx of sincere, brown-faced bird-watchers and naturalists of both sexes, and three bored-looking local reporters. The rest of the seats were filled by the villagers, some who had come for the entertainment value and some who wanted to object. These last were mostly, as Mr. Fairfax had prophesied, the people who had bought country cottages to retire to. Paul settled back in his seat, feeling depressed and nervous. Gus was picking at the woodworm holes in the pillar, with a nail. He had already described the people on the platform with a selection from his new, uninhibited vocabulary, excepting Sydney as an afterthought.

At ten past eight the chairman, looking rather worried, opened the meeting by introducing the people on the platform. He said how fortunate they were to be able to welcome Mr. August Cartwright to the village, and that he was too well known to need any introduction. He then introduced him at great length, listing all his publications ('I bet old Cartwright put him up to this,' Gus muttered to Paul), and eventually called upon the distinguished visitor to open the meeting by giving a short address.

'Open it?' Gus muttered. 'That's half an hour gone already.'

Mr. August Cartwright got to his sensibly shod feet to a spattering of polite applause. Paul noticed that a lot of the bird-watchers only made two claps for the sake of convention, but that the Colonel Spiggott brigade clapped very heartily. Gus didn't clap at all. He was picking at the worm-holes again.

Mr. Cartwright had a plummy voice and spoke with emotion about 'our defiled coasts' and the 'inroads of the speculator'. He talked about the good old days of the country squire, who gave work and succour to the villagers ('Peasants, mate, peasants,' Gus muttered) and the sad break-up of the ancestral homes of England. Paul couldn't see what it all had to do with Birdsmarsh and had an unpleasant feeling that what Gus was now muttering was true: 'Load of old crap.'

'But to come to the particular,' Mr. Cartwright boomed, 'this sweet corner of the Essex coast, as yet unspoilt, a haven of peace, is now threatened with "amenities" in the shape of a marina for yachts.'

'What else does he think a marina's for? Rubber ducks?'

Paul began to wish he hadn't insisted on Gus's coming with him.

'This is not an amenity for the village. This is an amenity for yachtsmen, an invitation to the outboard-motor horde to come racketing up and down our peaceful waterfront. It's no amenity for the lovely old farm of Birdsmarsh, mentioned in the Domesday Book . . .'

'It's an amenity for your old man, though,' Gus said to Paul. 'All that lolly.'

Paul frowned. Somehow Mr. Cartwright sounded all wrong, in spite of the fact that he was saying what Paul thought he believed. And Birdsmarsh wasn't a lovely old farm, and it wasn't mentioned in the Domesday Book. But when at last Mr. Cartwright sat down and one of the naturalists got to his feet

Paul felt that he was on firmer ground. The naturalist spoke very sensibly, in a flat unemotional voice, listing the rare birds that had been seen at Birdsmarsh, and making a plea for the marina to be re-sited in an area where there was a yacht centre already. Mr. Cartwright boomed, 'Hear, hear', in patronizing tones, and the naturalist gave him a cold look as he sat down. Somebody then asked just what the marina was going to entail, and Mr. Glass's solicitor answered with the description from his papers which was all too familiar to Paul: the lock-gates and basin, concrete promenade, hotel, club-house, chandlers' shops, refuelling station and car park for a thousand cars. When he had sat down, Colonel Spiggott jumped to his feet and started decrying the 'intrusion of this concrete-and-glass monstrosity into our midst', and Mr. Cartwright had another unctuous declamation about 'our heritage', to be followed by various well-preserved ladies in suède jackets extolling the 'loveliness' of the estuary. None of them, Paul thought, had ever been seen beyond the limits of the village street and their tastefully planted cottage gardens; they did their shopping by Mini in Maldon and never put a brogue near the harbour mud. As the 'hear, hears' went on, and the County Council men muffled polite yawns behind their papers, Gus went on picking at the wooden pillar with his nail. He had stopped making remarks, and did not look sarcastic any more, only angry.

Mrs. Spiggott, the Colonel's wife, finished her piece and the chairman looked pointedly at his watch. Everybody looked round, satisfied with the evening's effort and the atmosphere of righteous indignation that had been created. Paul felt resigned and inadequate—against the plan, but against the Colonel Spiggotts and their tribe, too, and the unctuousness of the professional country-lover, Mr. August Cartwright. He was surprised when Gus suddenly got to his feet beside him. He thought he was going to walk out, and half got up to follow him, but to his surprise Gus glared at the chairman and said in a loud voice, 'Sir, this isn't right.'

Everyone turned round and stared. The chairman nodded at Gus to proceed, and Gus, a high colour in his cheeks and his eyes very sharp and angry, said, 'There's another side to this.' He hesitated a moment, as if suddenly realizing what he had taken on, then, aware of the expectant silence, he said, 'Nobody who has spoken here tonight is a working person. Birdsmarsh isn't—isn't Frinton or something. It's a working village that's died because the work's left it—the barges and the fishing and all that. It's all right for Mr. Cartwright and Mrs. Spiggott and them to talk about keeping it unspoilt, but what about the real village people—the ones that didn't choose to live here, but who had the rotten luck to be born here? What are they supposed to do for work? The only thing that's ever come along that looks like providing work for the village, and you get all this stuff about "our heritage". Well, work's a heritage, isn't it? What good's a village without work? You ask a few of the people that belong here, and they won't go on about spoiling the place.'

There was a sharp, embarrassed silence. The County Council men and Mr. Glass's solicitor were smiling and looking interested for the first time during the evening; Mr. Cartwright looked angry and Mrs. Spiggott's face had gone tight with insult, the make-up standing out unbecomingly. The chairman looked round, and cleared his throat awkwardly.

'Well, I think we have had a very interesting evening's discussion . . .' It was obvious that he did not want an argument to develop at this late stage, and he wound the meeting up with far more agility than he had opened it. A buzz of interested conversation broke out as the platform took its leave and the meeting broke up, and Gus growled at Paul, 'I must have gone mad. Let's get out of here.'

He shoved his way towards the door, aware of interested stares from all sides. Everybody knew Gus; nobody had been able to think up an answer to his argument in time to present it to the chairman and a great many were honest enough to acknowledge the truth of what he had said. Mrs. Spiggott, having been mentioned by name, blocked his way on the path outside, and when Gus tried to pass she caught his arm and said, 'Gus Roper, I should have said you were the last person to stand up and talk about wanting work. As a governor of the school I know it was only too obvious that work was the last thing you were interested in.'

Paul thought, looking at her, 'What a beast the woman is.' He stood by Gus, afraid of what Gus would say, feeling very loyal to him in spite of what he had said. He thought of Gus getting Chris out of the water, and he looked at Mrs. Spiggott and saw the hardness of her face and the vanity that decked out her skin and narrow lips.

'I'm not at school now,' Gus said menacingly.

To Paul's intense relief, Sydney loomed up beside them and said placatingly to Mrs. Spiggott, 'Well, we did our best, eh? Let's hope our opinions will carry some weight.' He turned to Gus and Paul. 'How's that ocean racer of yours getting on, you two? I see you're getting down to work on her.'

'Work?' said Gus. Paul kicked him sharply on the ankle, and as Mrs. Spiggott disappeared into the dusk Sydney sighed and shook his head. He had prevented an argument and didn't want to start another by saying anything provocative to Gus. He could see that Gus was in an angry mood, looking very much like his father as he stood there in the dusk, glowering after Mrs. Spiggott.

Paul said, 'I don't suppose anything will come of objecting.' It was half statement, half a question.

'We'll see,' Sydney said. 'The County Council have promised a decision by September.' He paused. 'You must excuse me. I'm driving back to London with Mr. Cartwright.' He looked slightly embarrassed. Paul guessed that he didn't like Mr. Cartwright and his professional country-loving. He wouldn't have spoken to them if he hadn't seen that they needed protection from Mrs. Spiggott. They said good night, and walked down the village street towards the harbour.

Gus had hunched his shoulders and pushed his hands into his pockets, and Paul didn't want to provoke his wrath any further. Besides, now there was no common ground between them. Gus had spoken openly of what he wanted for Birdsmarsh, and Paul, admiring his courage, could scarcely admire his sentiments. Yet it was right for him, Paul thought. It was more right for Gus to want it, than it was for the Mrs. Spiggott tribe not to want it. At this point in his thinking Paul recognized his own confusion, and sighed heavily.

Gus said, 'You going tomorrow? On *Woodwind*, I mean?'

'Yes.'

Gus grunted. They came to his gate and he said briefly, 'See you,' and turned up the garden path.

Cross and disappointed, Paul turned back to a track that ran behind the village towards the farm, and set off for home. He felt needled by Gus's behaviour and their unfriendly parting and told himself that he was glad Gus couldn't come on *Woodwind*. 'Serve him jolly well right,' he thought. The meeting had been a farce, he decided. Nothing was any good. The track came out on to the drive up to Birdsmarsh, and as he came to it Paul was surprised by the headlights of a car coming from the farm. He backed into the hedge, and the car pulled up beside him. It was Chris driving his father's Land-Rover.

'I'm just going over to Peter's to see that it's all right for tomorrow. I only got home half an hour ago. Want to come?'

'All right.'

The large suitcase with Charlie in it was on the front seat, and Chris stood it up and pulled it towards him to make room.

'I thought we could put this on board tonight. Save trouble in the morning. How did the meeting go?'

'Oh, all right,' Paul said grudgingly.

'Who did the protesting?' Chris eased the clutch and the Land-Rover lurched on down the drive.

'Mrs. Spiggott and people like that. The bird-watchers were all right. It was pretty dull, really.' He didn't say anything about Gus's speech. From the way he spoke it was obvious that he didn't want to say anything much about it at all. Chris, who had only inquired out of kindness, was glad to change the subject.

'You're coming tomorrow, aren't you?'

'Yes.'

'We're leaving at midday. That's high water. Mr. Warner's coming, too, Peter told me. That suits me, because it makes two responsible witnesses. If the test is a success, that is.'

'Nothing's going to happen like that time with *Swannie?*' Paul said anxiously. 'Why do you say *if* it's a success? What can go wrong?'

'It's highly unlikely I'll hit anything again,' Chris said. 'So don't worry about that. But in experiments like this you just get a bit wary about assuming everything's going to go as it should. You can't help qualifying everything with "if". I suppose because it means so much to me, to prove it.'

'Why, what does it mean?'

'Vindication of a couple of years' very hard work, for a start. The usual lift anyone gets when something they believe in works out right. And also, commercially it could make me independent. If it's proved, I can sell the idea to a firm like Dunfort's. I don't say it'll make me a fortune, but it might make all the difference between being able to choose the sort of job I want in a year or two and having to grab the first thing that's offered.'

Paul was silent. His own troubles seemed a woolly mess beside Chris's pointed ambition. Chris hadn't a trace of sentiment in his nature. He hadn't even the imagination to be frightened of what he was going to do. Paul sighed.

'You're a terrible worrier, aren't you?' Chris said kindly.

'Well, you never saw what you looked like that other time,' Paul said indignantly.

Chris laughed. 'No. You've got a point there.'

Paul qualified his remark. 'I suppose it must have felt pretty ghastly, though.'

'Yes. That's why I don't intend it to happen again. That's the whole point of getting *Woodwind* to come along, instead of just launching myself into a tidal stream and waiting till I land up somewhere. Proctor's contention is that that would be the proper way to do this test. But he won't volunteer to be the guinea-pig.'

'Huh.'

They called at the Research Station and met Peter Winnington and his uncle, Mr. Warner, whom Winnington called Willy. Paul thought him a rather grim-looking man with his rimless spectacles and iron-grey hair. He had a quiet manner, but there was an authority about him that Paul recognized with a further sinking of his heart. He didn't feel any happier at the prospect of going through this ordeal with such a pair for company. He still didn't like Winnington and was convinced that he was a liar. Watching him as they drove down to the harbour to put the suit on board, along with water and provisions, Paul thought that he seemed ill at ease. He smoked continuously and did not make conversation with his usual charm; in fact, he was unusually silent, almost absent-minded. Paul sat squashed against him in the Aston Martin, aware of him out of the corner of his eye, breathing in the fumes of the cigarette smoke and fancying himself as a detective. Afterwards, when he was driving back to the farm with Chris in the Land-Rover, Paul told Chris about the night Winnington had gone on board *Swannie*, after the accident.

'But Gus asked him and he said he never did.'

'Then he didn't, presumably,' Chris said.

'But it was him,' Paul said.

'You're not insinuating that he's a thief, or a liar?'

'I think he is a liar. It was him.'

'God, what a time to start telling tales like that!' Chris said, suddenly angry.

'I'm not telling tales. I'm only saying something,' Paul said doggedly.

'Well, you'd do better to keep your mouth shut if that's all you can find to say. If you didn't actually see him on board, you can't go round saying he's a liar. If you feel like that about him, you'd better stay at home tomorrow.'

'Oh, but I can't now,' Paul said involuntarily.

'Then for Pete's sake don't go round making remarks like that.'

Paul was already wondering why he hadn't accepted his chance of forgoing the journey. Chris was annoyed with him and said no more for the rest of the drive, and Paul sat sullenly watching the insects zooming across the beam of the headlights. It was late. Paul, who had dreaded this date with *Woodwind*, now clung like a limpet to his right to go. He felt that his presence on board was quite vital, but exactly why, he had no idea.

8

'WOODWIND' AT SEA

Woodwind lifted her fine bows to the swell as the sea-walls fell away astern. Paul sat on her foredeck listening to the hiss of the water along her sides, trying not to be impressed by the speed with which she slipped along. The wind was light from the south, the sky cloudless. 'Everything is perfect,' Paul thought nervously. In the clear light of day he was realizing that he had done the wrong thing last night in telling Chris that he thought Peter Winnington was a liar. 'What a fool I am,' he thought, watching the marbled patterns of the foam sliding away below him. He remembered the look on Gus's face when he had stood up to state his case, and recognized again that Gus had courage. He remembered Chris calling him a worrier, and he looked at the glittering horizon and thought, 'How stupid I am, to be sitting here and thinking of things that are done and no good thinking about any more. Plenty to worry about, anyway, with what's coming.' The light made his eyes water and he put his glasses on. The horizon sharpened, as perfect a summer horizon as the North Sea ever offered, with a coaster putting up a pencil of smoke and, above, an aeroplane repeating the line with a vapour trail like a dropped thread on blue silk. Paul thought of Gus chipping at the mud and rust underneath Reg Mason's lorries, and sighed.

Woodwind was travelling fast. The sea was calm, the wind fair and steady. The radio was on so that they wouldn't forget the weather forecast, and the three men in the cockpit were chatting above a cricket commentary from Lord's. Glancing back, Paul saw Chris looking very relaxed and unafraid, a mug of tea in his hand. Winnington was at the tiller, smiling in a distant sort of way at something his uncle was saying. Paul had been struck again by Peter Winnington's reserve. He had spoken very little, and still looked abstracted and slightly worried, as he had been the night before. Paul had the impression that he was as nervous about the trip as he was himself, but could think of no reason why he should be. He was an experienced enough sailor, and had no real responsibility for Chris; for it was Chris who had asked him to take him. Chris had even signed a paper and

given it to Mr. Warner, absolving him from any responsibility in the case of accident: a mere formality to Chris's methodical way of thinking, but to Paul, who had caught sight of it accidentally, a gruesome ritual that had considerably increased his unease.

'We'll be half-way to Holland by the time the tide turns, at this rate,' Warner was saying. 'You can start your testing plumb in the middle of the North Sea.'

'Ideal,' Chris said. 'Pity it's so warm, though. It should be January really.'

'There's nothing to stop you testing again in January, if you're successful this time.'

'No. That's true.'

Chris was scheduled to go overboard at six in the evening, when the tide turned, and to stay overboard for twenty-four hours. The prospect obviously did not worry him. Paul tried not to think about it. He looked up at the sails and the hot sky, and felt the deck warm beneath his jeans. *Woodwind* moved without any fuss, scarcely heeled, spewing a white foam from her stem that rode the accompanying waves and dissolved into bubbles astern. The water was dark, not any colour at all that Paul could put a name to. Looking down into it, it looked infinitely powerful, and suggested to Paul feelings and fears and beauties that he knew could not be expressed in words at all. But looking out to the horizon it looked like a jolly poster for British Rail, all sun and glitter and invitation, with the aeroplane drawing arcs of vapour, and northward the blobs of the beach huts and the diamond sparks of reflection from Clacton pier. Paul looked at his watch. It was two o'clock. He shifted his position slightly to keep out of the shadow thrown by the staysail, leaned his head on his arms and waited for the evening to come.

At two o'clock Gus wriggled into the black gloom underneath the sagging guts of a coal lorry and started to chip viciously at the solidified dirt under its chassis. A couple of feet to the side the sun glared down on the concrete, but underneath the lorry the concrete was like the marble of a mortuary slab. Gus was now accustomed to oily incarceration beneath lorries, and the dull ache of lifted arms no longer had to power to make him swear, but as his scraper started raining down the dirt he could see nothing but *Woodwind* reaching out to sea in the sparkling sun. He had never supposed that he had much imagination, but beneath the lorry he could feel the easy motion of the yacht as if he were standing on her foredeck at that very moment; he could see, looking down from her pulpit, the untroubled bow-wave she turned over and the foam trailing faintly out across the swell. He jabbed the scraper up into the darkness. The darkness and the dirt matched his discontent; his longing to be on board *Woodwind* was a stronger emotion than he had ever experienced before; his frustration in the black prison beneath the lorry worse than any physical pain he could think of. The vision of the white yacht would not leave him. As he worked he got hot and the dried dirt stuck to the sweat on his face and worked itself into his eyes and was gritty in his mouth, and all the time he could see *Woodwind* lifting to the gentle southerly, and the reflection of the water dappling her white counter and the gold-incised letters of her name, and the streamers of disturbed water like revolving dimples in her wake. His eyes watered with the irritation of the dirt and he began to think he was crying for longing for *Woodwind*, and the more he thought about it the more reason he saw there was for crying at his plight when he might have been on the yacht. But he wasn't a child any longer; in fact, he had never felt more old and sane in his life and there was no relief in tears any longer. The only relief he would get would come with knocking-off time. He would ride home on his bike and go down to the harbour, and it would be dead low water. *Phoebe* and *Emma* and *Swannie* would be angled on the mud, squat and black like old stranded crabs, but out at sea, the late sun gold on her sails, *Woodwind* would still be travelling eastward. Gus felt the lungs in his chest contract with longing. Or was it the dust that choked him? He eased himself farther into the dank cave beneath the lorry and went on chipping and longing, and swearing softly with his gritty tongue.

'I don't think the tide will take you to any shore from here,' Mr. Warner said to Chris, 'not for some weeks, at any rate. If you go overboard now, there'll be no trouble about getting washed up before your test's complete.'

'Good,' Chris said. 'I'll get going, then.'

This was the moment Paul had dreaded. He saw Winnington at the tiller reach into his anorak pocket for his cigarettes and glance at his uncle as he did so, half inquiringly. Chris went below to change into his woollen underwear, and Paul sat on the cabin-top watching Winnington. Now that the moment had come Paul found that he was almost trembling if he did not keep a conscious restraint on his limbs. He could not get out of his head the knowledge that Winnington was a liar, and somehow he could not convince himself that it wouldn't affect Chris, launched on his hazardous experiment. And at the same time as he felt the trembling in his knees, the same part of his character was scoffing at the hallucinations, and saying with infinite scorn, 'What a fool you are! What a girl. What a nit.' He got up and went below to Chris, trying not to let his worry show.

'All right?' Chris queried. He was pulling thick socks on over the legs of the underpants.

Paul nodded. It was when Chris was gone, and he was responsible for keeping him within sight, that he dreaded. He could not believe that Winnington was going to bother at all.

'I'm pretty lucky having a boat like this to do it from,' Chris said, for the sake of something to say. He thought Paul looked rather sick. 'Why don't you take a pill?' he asked kindly. 'There are some in the first-aid kit, and they work marvellously.'

'What for?' said Paul. 'I'm all right.'

'I thought you looked a bit green.'

'I'm not sick. I just wish it were over, that's all.'

'You're not worrying about me?' Chris asked, amazed. He stared at Paul as if he were something off another planet. 'Good God, Paul, you're worse than a mother hen.' He pulled a second jersey over his head. 'That accident isn't likely to repeat itself, you know. Come on, I thought you'd enjoy the trip. Stop being such a nit.' He was half-teasing, half-serious. Paul could see that he was excited and happy himself, his eyes shining with his inventor's fervour. 'Help me on with Charlie and I can get started.'

Having something to do was a help, Paul found. If only there was going to be something more he could do than merely watch for the next twenty-four hours the prospect would have pleased him more. He helped Chris do up the zippers and buckles and inflate the outer layer of the suit until he looked like the circus fat man, cumbersome and ridiculous in the small cabin. Even Paul had to smile as Chris struck a ballet stance on one dimpled leg.

'You'd have to harpoon me before I sank in this lot,' he said.

He eased himself carefully out into the cockpit. Winnington had backed the staysail so that *Woodwind* lay hove-to, lifting easily to the swell, but not making any way. Winnington and Warner both looked at Chris critically, not amused, but appraising—almost, Paul thought, respectful. The sun was still a good way above the horizon; it was a warm and perfect evening, the sea burnished and glittering to the horizon in every direction. There was no sight of land, and no other vessel to be seen.

'Conditions are perfect for us,' Warner said with a smile. 'But too good for you, I suppose? Scarcely Arctic.'

'No. But we can prove the mechanics of the thing. After all, a test purely for heat preservation could be done in a tank, if necessary.'

'That's true.'

Chris pulled the tight hood up over his head, and zipped up the mittens over his hands. 'All right,' he said. 'That's everything.'

'We'll keep by you then. And we'll give you the lamp when it goes dark. Good luck.'

Chris climbed carefully over the lifelines and let himself fall backwards with a hollow flop like an animated air-bed. He floated high, sliding gently with *Woodwind*, feet first down the waves. Paul looked at him doubtfully. *Woodwind* went away from him very slowly, hardly at all, and it was clear that he would have no difficulty in keeping by her. He waved cheerfully.

'We're off.'

'We'll keep a log for you,' Mr. Warner said. He glanced at his watch. 'Five forty-five exactly. Better put the radio on, Pete, so we get the forecast,' he added. He looked at Paul. 'Are you taking first watch, Paul? We only want one on now. I'll make some supper and Peter can get some sleep in when he's eaten.'

'You've nothing to do for the boat,' Peter Winnington said to Paul. 'She'll look after herself. Just watch Chris, and keep an eye open for any traffic.'

'All right.'

Paul sat down beside the tiller. It was lashed, and jerked mutinously every now and then like a chained dog. The sea was still calm, the sun hot. Paul put his feet up and tried to relax. 'It's all right now,' he thought. It was almost, he supposed, enjoyable. Chris was just a couple of yards away; there was a delicious smell of cooking wafting out of the galley. Paul looked at the horizon, half-closing his eyes until the brightness blended and sparks of dazzling light elongated into spears, filling his vision. The sun was hanging from the spreaders of the yacht, reassuringly high, and the motion was infinitesimal. It was five to six. Ten minutes, Paul thought, out of twenty-four hours.

'Have they got the radio on?' Chris asked. 'For the forecast?'

'Yes,' Paul said. He could hear someone singing, which was assuredly neither Warner nor Winnington. It was slimy, old-fashioned swing music which set his teeth on edge, not decent music, not even decent with-it pop. It seemed ridiculous to be listening to a full band and vocal in the middle of the ocean, part of a minute speck of civilization trespassing in the basic elements of air and water, uninvited, unrespected. The situation was completely unreal, yet taken for granted by the others. Winnington had a frying-pan in his hand and was carefully levering an omelette on to its uncooked side, his tongue tipped between his lips with concentration. His hair was a mass of curls in the sea air, not neat and tidy as it was at home, and his face was flushed with the day's sun. Paul knew he ought to like him, but he couldn't.

'Super smell,' Chris said.

'Are you supposed to be having any?' Paul asked. Surely it was too much, he thought, for Chris to eat an omelette with a knife and fork in his situation.

'No, I'm going to do with as little as possible. But it's going to be hard, if I'm going to be subjected to aromas like that.'

'I'll tell you what it tastes like,' Paul said, as a plate of bacon and omelette was passed out to him.

'Is he complaining already?' Winnington asked from below.

Eating his meal, which tasted marvellous, Paul remembered Gus again, with a pang of guilt. Almost, now, he was enjoying it. The evening was very calm and golden, and seemed to take a long time. Paul felt as if he were waiting for whatever it was he dreaded to happen, but he could no longer visualize what it was he dreaded. Chris was a mere ten yards away; he kept up with *Woodwind*'s slightly faster drift by swimming idly at intervals to catch her up. For the rest of the time he lay dozing or humming. Below, Winnington and his uncle were both lying on the bunks in the saloon.

The sun went down into the sea, splashing with a splendid Victorian extravagance of red and purple the underbellies of drifting cloud above the horizon, and Paul realized suddenly that the air was cool and that a star was tipping the spreaders now, and that the soft breeze was beginning to whine slightly in the shrouds. Peter Winnington got up from his bunk and switched the light on below. Paul saw him stretch, and reach for his jersey.

'I'll come up and give you a break,' he said. 'We should be getting a bit more wind shortly, according to the forecast.'

Paul's new content faded abruptly. Already, now that the sun had gone, the sea was uninviting and hostile.

'You can turn in, if you like,' Winnington said, as he came out into the cockpit. He went up on deck to check that the navigation lights were on, and then stood leaning on the shrouds, looking down at Chris.

'The sea's getting up a bit,' he remarked.

'Yes, so I've noticed.'

'The forecast was force five for this area. It won't be so comfortable if it materializes.'

'Ah, well . . .' Chris was non-committal. He looked comfortable enough at the moment. 'I'd better have that light on. Will you pass it down?'

Winnington went below again and Paul sat on in the cockpit, beside the restless tiller. Chris was hard to see in the half-light, blue-black and faintly shining like the sea itself. He said to Paul, 'If Peter can't find it, tell him it's in that zip bag of mine.'

'He has found it,' Paul said. He could see Winnington with it in his hand. He had his back to the cockpit and was unscrewing something. Paul thought he was changing the bulb. His uncle was still lying on the bunk, and saying something in a low voice which Paul could not catch. Paul heard Winnington say, 'That should fix it.'

He came back into the cockpit, and Chris paddled himself alongside and took the lamp. It was small but powerful enough for the job, worked by a sealed battery, and Chris slipped it over his head on a strap, so that it shone from his forehead like a miner's lamp. Its bright beam cheered Paul up considerably.

'All set for the night watch,' Winnington said. 'I'll take over, Paul. You go and get some sleep.'

Paul went below, aware suddenly that he was tired, but convinced that he wouldn't be able to go to sleep. Warner was still lying on the bunk, apparently dozing. Relieved that he didn't have to make conversation, Paul slipped between the blankets on the opposite bunk and turned his back on Warner, so that he could pretend to sleep and not have to say anything if Warner got up. It was warm and comfortable and Paul was sorry for Chris.

The next thing he remembered was hitting his head against the locker as *Woodwind* rolled uncomfortably into a trough. He half-turned, startled, muffled with the blankets and unable to remember for a few seconds where he was. Then, as he opened his eyes, he saw the neat cabin and the rumpled empty blankets on the opposite bunk, and he heard the wind whining outside. He turned his head and knew that he was terribly afraid. The fear went through him like a sharp pain. He threw off the blankets and stumbled out on to the cabin floor. The boat was sailing; he could feel the motion all round him and hear the strong tune of the wind. He heard a cry from somewhere outside, and the grinding whirr of the sheet-winch.

'Chris!'

He did not wait to wonder why he was afraid. He shot out of the cabin, scrambling up into the darkness out of the hatch. He saw Peter Winnington's face staring at him, furious and wet with spray.

'Where's Chris? Oh, where is he?'

Woodwind was no longer hove-to, but sailing furiously into what seemed like wild, buffeting space. There was no light shining in the darkness around her, only the coloured glow of her navigation lights up in the shrouds. Paul stared at Winnington and his uncle. Warner was hunched up in oilskins, looking out over the stern, but Winnington was leaning over Paul, his eyes startled, saying, 'For God's sake, what do you want?'

'Where is Chris? Where is he?' Paul grasped Winnington's arm and shook it hysterically. 'Why are we sailing? Where is he?' He heard his own voice, shrill and screaming, and did not care. He wanted to shake honesty out of Winnington, screw the answers from his scornful mouth. Winnington's hand closed over his arm and held it in a furious grip.

'For God's sake, you young idiot!' he hissed. He threw Paul's arm off, nearly knocking him back into the cabin. 'We're picking him up, you fool!'

'What's gone wrong? Where's the light?' Paul sobbed. 'You've lost him! I heard him shouting, and now you've lost him!'

Winnington did not reply, but pushed the tiller over to go about. Warner swung round and said roughly, 'You're weak! You're a fool!' and Winnington said to him very curtly, 'Make the sheet fast!' The mainsail flogged briefly overhead, and Paul heard the rasping whirr of the winch again. The wind brought spray with it, spattering over his face. He did not know what was happening, only that in his sleep he had heard Chris cry out and his fear was so acute that he felt no shame with it. He would have attacked Winnington like a fighting cat if he had not turned back for Chris; he still had an insane desire to shout at him, to scream for Chris into the wind, and rail at *Woodwind* for her negligence.

'Where is Chris's light? Do you know where he is?' His voice quavered, only just under control.

Winnington did not reply. He was sailing *Woodwind* close to the wind, pinching her up. Paul leaned over the coaming, staring into the darkness, shaking with this terrible fear that was now becoming a familiar thing. The sea was no longer the starlit sheet of calm water he had last seen, but a mass of white-flicked, choppy waves that tumbled and dropped drunkenly under *Woodwind*'s hull. She pitched through it, throwing water up over her bows which came down into the cockpit like rain. Paul knew they could never see Chris without his light, only perhaps hear him shout. *Woodwind*'s own lights were there for him to see, if he could. Paul already thought Chris was drowned again and the image of the bluish, lifeless face was in every wave.

'*Woodwind!* Ahoy!'

The voice was thin on the wind, but quite close.

'Back the staysail!' Winnington snapped to his uncle. Paul's heart had leapt like a startled gull, almost choking him.

'Chris!'

'Here, over to your right!'

'Starboard bow,' Winnington said. He had checked *Woodwind*'s wild plunging by getting her hove-to once more. She ducked to the waves and rolled slightly, but made no way. Paul could see Chris's face shining faintly.

'I'm coming aboard!' he shouted.

Winnington said something softly to his uncle, and then called across the water, 'We're hove-to. Come across!'

The next minute Chris was reaching up and grasping the edge of the deck, and Paul leaned over and grasped his wrist. He did not dare say anything; he did not want to give his panic away yet again.

'It's not only that darned light,' Chris said to Winnington. 'But I'm making water. It's no good going on, else the same thing will happen that happened before. I was getting a bit anxious until I saw you coming back.'

'We overshot,' Winnington said. 'You were some way away when the light went out. Sorry if we gave you a scare.'

He was helping Chris up over the lifelines. Paul shrank back into the hatch, biting his lip to stop himself saying anything stupid. He had already said enough. He felt drained of feeling now, cold and angry with himself. Chris was swearing softly to himself as he unzippered the suit.

'I can't understand the ruddy thing. Oh, for Pete's sake, the wretched, blasted thing . . .'

'Leave it till daylight,' Winnington said. 'You must be famished.'

He had *Woodwind* sailing again, and was checking her course on the chart. Paul saw his face in the binnacle light, very grim and astonishingly pale. Or was it the greenish cast of the light?

But the voices—even Chris's swearing—were unexcited. Paul shuddered. The fear had been like a wild animal inside him, and now it was being shown up for what it was: girl's hysterics. Paul's shame silenced him utterly. He backed down into the cabin and sat on the bunk with his head in his hands. *Woodwind* was sailing again, and he felt seasick. He felt sick, physically, and even sicker in his mind. He couldn't stop shivering.

When Chris had divested himself of the suit he came below and Winnington followed him and put the kettle on in the galley. Chris was drawn and angry with disappointment and slumped on the bunk opposite Paul. Winnington got out a bottle of brandy and some glasses. Paul noticed that his hands were shaking, and was surprised.

'I'm sorry to waste your time,' Chris said to him.

'Don't talk like that. I'm sorry that we couldn't have guaranteed things going right.'

'Oh—I've got to expect snags,' Chris growled. 'But I can't understand this particular one. Of all the things that might have happened, this wasn't one I'd thought of. I thought I'd cleared up the leaks long ago. After all, the light failing was nothing. I wouldn't have chucked it in just for that.'

'I'll get you something to eat and you can bed down.' Winnington glanced at his watch. 'It's four o'clock, you know. It's just beginning to go light. You haven't done so badly.'

He made strong coffee and they all drank it topped up with brandy. Paul felt he needed it. Winnington did not look at him or speak to him and Chris was only concerned with his own trouble. Paul was glad that he could nurse his raw feelings in peace. He finished his coffee and lay down on the bunk, otherwise he knew he would have been sick. He pulled the blanket over his head and felt a great relief at being hidden, in darkness, alone. He wanted to go to sleep and forget his shame, but the strong coffee and the brandy decided otherwise. Long after Winnington had gone back into the cockpit and Chris was asleep on the opposite bunk Paul was still going over the incident in his mind. The more he dwelled on the sequence of events, the more strange it all seemed in his head, until he wasn't sure what was the brandy and what was the truth and what his imagination. But why had Winnington been so fierce and so frightened, and why had he been sailing away from Chris? Paul was haunted by the furious eyes that had raked him in the cockpit. In his memory they were fanatically angry, uncivilized eyes, lit by an agony of mind that Paul had never seen before. The brandy was like fire in his stomach. 'Why,' Paul said to himself, 'you're drunk!' But it did not calm him. Why, he wondered, had he woken up just when things had started going wrong, as if it were an instinct that had aroused him? Why had *Woodwind* been sailing, instead of lying hove-to? But Chris, asleep, was unworried. His face was smooth and untroubled and his breath came evenly. He had not seemed to think anything strange had been going on. Paul wondered if it was all his own feverish imagination playing him tricks, even if, perhaps, Winnington wasn't a liar after all. He slept heavily and awoke to bright sunshine, feeling as if he were coming up from the bottom of a deep mine. His head ached abominably. Chris was sitting opposite him, eating baked beans and bacon. The smell turned Paul's stomach.

'Hiya,' Chris said, without expression.

'Where are we?'

'Pete says we'll be home in a couple of hours.'

Paul turned over on to his back and lay looking up at the deck beams. Through the portholes reflections of the water rippled up across the roof in a soothing flickering movement; *Woodwind* was sailing easily with only a slight, steady heel, and Paul could hear the water chuckling beside his ear. It was very pleasant, just for a moment.

'What are you going to do?' he said to Chris, when he remembered.

'Do? Oh, heaven knows. I haven't thought yet.' He ate the rest of his breakfast and said, 'Do you want a cup of tea?'

'Yes, please.'

Chris filled another mug and then said, 'I'll go back to Cambridge and try to clear up this leaking before Proctor goes away on holiday. I can't understand the darned thing at all. It was quite impossible for it to fail the way it did.' He passed the mug over to Paul, who propped himself up on one elbow. 'Then I think I might go to Bavaria with Proctor. He's been asking me and I kept saying no, but now . . .' Chris shrugged. 'I'd probably feel more like tackling the whole thing again after a holiday.'

Paul sipped the tea, trying not to think about last night. If Gus had been aboard, he thought, he wouldn't have been so scared. But what had he been so scared about? In the broad light of day it was hard to remember.

9
THE SMACK RACE

Two men stood up on the sea-wall. They had coloured poles that they had stuck in a straight course across the marshes. A theodolite on its tripod stood like a contemplative heron on the wall, and one of the men was writing busily in a notebook.

'If you object to them so strenuously,' Gus said to Paul, 'why don't you chuck 'em off? It's your land.'

'They got permission off Dad, so how can I?'

Paul and Gus were sprawled on *Swannie*'s deck, eating crisps. Gus had a day off work after working overtime over the week-end and had come down to *Swannie* with the intention of moving her out of her berth at high water and putting her on the hard beach, so that he could do her bottom ready for the race. There were still two hours to go before she would float, and Gus wasn't sorry to be doing nothing. The sun was hot. He had his shirt off and lay with his hands behind his head, staring up at the sky, amused at Paul's attitude to the surveyors.

'They're ahead of themselves anyway,' Paul growled. 'How do they know they're going to get permission?'

'They soon *will* know,' Gus said. 'One way or the other, at least,' he added tactfully.

'Huh.' Paul would have been quite happy if the surveyors hadn't arrived on the scene. It was like old times with Gus, pottering. The strains in their relationship seemed to have dissolved, nothing more had been said about the night of the objectors' meeting, and Gus hadn't even been funny about not going on *Woodwind*. He seemed to have accepted it now, as part of his inevitable fate.

'Is Chris going to test again? On *Woodwind*, I mean?' Gus said. 'I suppose he'll have to, if the thing was a failure.'

'He was terribly fed up,' Paul said. He had thought about the night on *Woodwind* a great deal during the week that followed, and had convinced himself that something odd had been happening when he woke up. Chris, preoccupied with the failure of the suit, hadn't seemed to have laid any great significance on the fact that *Woodwind* had sailed away from him.

'Surely he was just getting the yacht sailing again, to come round and pick me up when the light failed?' he said, without heat. 'She wasn't very close when the light went out.'

Paul, remembering Chris's attitude when he had accused Winnington of being a liar, did not pursue the subject. But with Gus, now that they were friends again, it was different. He told him what had happened, in detail, only without saying what a panic he had been in.

Gus said affably, 'What are you getting at, then? You make it sound as if Winnington was going to leave him to it.'

'Yes, and with the suit leaking, that would have been the end for Chris.'

Gus blinked. He turned his head sideways and looked at Paul closely. Paul was watching the surveyors, his eyes thoughtful, his face very serious. His untidy yellow hair lifted in the breeze, showing a line of white where the sun hadn't tanned him, like the bleached shore that followed the foot of the seawall. Gus was worried.

'Have I got this right? You mean, Winnington was going to abandon Chris, and leave him to drown?'

'Yes. Winnington and his uncle. I think they tampered with the light to make it go out, and I'm not sure, but I think they also might have done something to the suit to make it leak.'

Gus sat up. He stared at Paul. 'Have you gone mad? You're not asking me to believe all this?'

'Well, you can believe what you like. I've just told you what happened. I've already told you that Winnington was on board *Swannie* that night. You didn't believe that, but it was the truth. Winnington can say what he likes. I think he's interested in the suit, and wants Chris out of the way. The night he went aboard *Swannie*, he examined the suit, perhaps made drawings of it.'

Gus was at a loss for words. He sat up abruptly and looked at Paul as if he had gone mad.

'You're not serious?'

'Of course I'm serious. I know you'll scoff at all this, and I wouldn't dare tell Chris, but nothing you can say will make me think otherwise.'

'Paul, you're mad.'

'I knew you'd say that.'

'Well, honestly. It's not the sort of thing that happens.'

'Not a lot, no. But it happens.'

'But surely most of your—your tale—is pure guesswork? I mean, what proof have you of all this?'

'I haven't any. That's why I can't go and tell the police, and I daren't even tell Chris. He'd be furious. He thinks Winnington is no end of a nice fellow.'

'But he is.'

'He was jolly nervous about the trip, right from the beginning. He didn't chat, or anything, like he usually does.'

'People don't feel like talking all the time. It just doesn't make sense, Paul.'

'It does to me. You can say what you like. You won't make me change my mind.'

Gus recognized Paul's stubbornness. He wanted to scoff and laugh at him, but the whole thing was beyond mere scoffing. To Gus, it was more evidence against Paul himself—Paul who, the last few months, had grown progressively moody and odd. Just because he had seen a man rowing in the harbour one moonlit midnight and convinced himself that it was Winnington coming from *Swannie*, he had built up a case of sabotage and attempted murder that would do credit to a thriller writer. Gus thought of Winnington, ordinary, familiar Winnington, with his well-pressed trousers and club tie and clean-cut British face, and tried to turn him into a murderer. But . . .

'Why, Winnington actually *saved* Chris's life!'

'Yes, I know,' Paul said stubbornly.

'Oh, Paul, you're cracked. You're not going to go round telling this stuff to anyone else, are you? It's dangerous.'

'No, of course not.'

'I'd forget it if I were you. Listen, you are coming on this smack race with me, aren't you? Last Saturday in August. Book the date.'

'Yes, I suppose so.'

'Good. Come on, then, let's get some work done.'

Gus didn't give Paul's theory another thought. They spent a thoroughly satisfactory afternoon scraping down one side of *Swannie*'s bottom and painting it with thick red anti-fouling that Gus had scrounged off a friendly smacksman. Even Paul enjoyed himself, feeling that he was beginning to like boats a bit more and understand their mystical ways. He was even beginning to pick up the jargon, and knew what Gus was talking about most of the time. Gus taught him to tie a bowline and a clove-hitch, and they strolled back along the sea-wall in the evening more content with each other's company than for several weeks. Gus dismissed Paul's lunacy from his mind; it was only a few days later when he was surprised by finding Chris aboard *Swannie* that he remembered all that had been said.

Chris was just coming up on deck when Gus jumped aboard. He grinned at Gus's startled expression.

'Sorry if I'm trespassing. I just came down to dump that old suit of mine in the hold. I want to do some more trials when I come back from holiday and this is as good a place to leave it as any. I don't want it hanging around at home, where someone might find it. It's not in your way, is it?'

'No, of course not.' Everything that Paul had said came back into Gus's head with a rush. He hesitated. 'You're sure it's—er—safe here?'

'Good Lord, whoever'd want to pinch it?'

'Oh, well—no, I suppose not.' Gus wanted to pursue the subject, to see if Chris had any suspicions about how Winnington had behaved, but he didn't quite know what to say. He said, tentatively, 'Is it all right now? Paul said it leaked.'

Chris's face clouded over. 'Yes, I've done a rough job on it, but it'll have to wait a bit longer for a proper going-over. The thing's still a complete mystery, how the leaks have come about.'

'It went all right until then? You kept with the yacht without any trouble?'

'Oh, yes. Or they kept with me, I suppose.'

Gus hesitated. 'Paul said he thought they were sailing away and leaving you at the end.' He felt guilty at saying it, but Paul's stubborn certainty was haunting.

Chris grinned. 'Poor old Paul! He gets het up over things, doesn't he? To tell you the truth, I thought they were for a minute. That's why I let out a bellow. I didn't admit it to Paul, though.'

'You'd already found that the suit was leaking?'

'Yes. I was getting lower and lower in the water, and my light had conked out, and then I saw the old yacht tearing off in the opposite direction, so naturally I let out a yell. And the boat turned round and came back and picked me up and I felt pretty relieved. I didn't say anything. I didn't want Peter to think I'd doubted his ability to look after me. After all, it was very decent of him to spend so much time helping me.'

Gus, suddenly, wondered why he did. Paul's suspicions were infectious.

'Have you patented this suit?' he asked.

'I've got a provisional patent—it's good for a year—but that's as far as I've got. After that it's hellish expensive—that's what puts me off. All my money gets eaten up by the suit as it is, and I owe Proctor nearly fifty pounds already. I'll have to do something about all this when I get back.'

'Get back from where?'

'From Bavaria. I'm going to stay with Proctor's ancient aunt in Mittenwald. Proctor swears it won't cost us a thing and we'll be fed like pigs on German sausages and cream cakes. I can't resist it.'

'When will you be back? I thought you might come on the

smack race with us.' Gus couldn't believe that anyone—Paul apart—might not leap at such an invitation.

'Why, what date is it?'

'Last Saturday in August.'

'That's the week-end we're coming home. I shan't be back till Sunday or Monday.'

'Oh, that's too late. Pity.'

Chris smiled. 'I hope you win, all the same.'

'Huh.' Gus did not want to talk about the subject dearest to his heart.

Later in the week Gus met Sydney Peacemaker. Sydney had come back from a sail in *Phoebe* and was sitting on his deck contemplating the warm tide that was lazily slipping down over the mud of Pewit Island. Skylarks shirred in the saltings. He could smell the warmed pitch of his own decks' caulking and the sour, salt mud that was uncovering all round him; out across the estuary the gulls cried and a Thames barge with brown topsail pulling was going out on the ebb, and it was as if everything about this muddy beloved harbour of his were conspiring to make him take notice, to impress upon his mind all the things that were so desirable about it: the peace, the smells, the funny little sandpipers pootling about to see what the ebb was revealing, the shimmer of the sun over the great grey breast of the estuary . . . and it was all doomed, in Sydney's knowledge, and the thought depressed him beyond all reason.

'Do you know,' he said to Gus, who rowed out to him and hung by one hand to the gunwale, 'the day before our smack race the Council are sitting to decide whether they should pass Mr. Glass's plans for Birdsmarsh. And on the morning of the race, which we are all looking forward to so much, I shall be sailing *Phoebe* and wondering what they have decided. And in my heart, for all we've tried to do, I feel sure that Mr. Glass is going to win, and every time I look forward to the smack race, all I can think of is—this . . .' His face was lined with anxiety like a bloodhound's.

Gus cleared his throat, slightly embarrassed. In his mind he was thinking, 'My holy aunt, what timing! Some crew Paul is going to make if the result is due in the village the same time the smacks are off.'

Dr. Peacemaker was looking at him with soulful eyes, and Gus guessed that he was seeing him as a dear old-fashioned fisherman's son, a native of the shore, tanned chest, thigh-boots and homespun, and he wanted to point out that he, the fisherman's son, wanted a concrete marina with all his heart. He didn't care if the skylarks migrated and the marshes glittered with the gaudy roofs of a thousand parked cars. He wanted the place to come alive. To his great relief, Sydney shook off his gloom and started to talk about the race, and then Gus was happy and in his element.

As the day of the race grew nearer, Gus had something else to worry about. His boss at work often had lorries in for attention at week-ends and increasingly Gus was asked to work on a Saturday or Sunday.

'And it's not really asking,' he complained to Paul. 'He just tells me. What if something crops up the race week-end?'

'You say you've got a prior engagement,' Paul said.

Gus scowled. 'I can just see his face.'

'You're not a slave, are you?' Paul said.

'Yes. Just about.'

'Get another job, then.'

'I wouldn't get another with the pay I'm getting now. It's only next Saturday I'm bothered about. I wouldn't complain otherwise. The faster I can save up some cash the sooner I can leave and do what I please.'

Paul shrugged. He was preoccupied with next Saturday for his own reasons. He could not believe that next Saturday it would all be decided. The fate of Birdsmarsh had dominated his thoughts for so long that he could scarcely imagine now what it would be like not to have to worry any more. For even if it was decided in Mr. Glass's favour, there would be no point in worrying any more. Not worrying, but . . . Paul tried to imagine how he would feel. He thought it would be as if Mr. Glass's bulldozers were to go to work on his own body, uprooting him from his land and leaving him without feelings or emotions. If he was not to have Birdsmarsh, he would have nothing. They could offer him anything in the world and his feelings would be like the dried-up roots of the countless trees Mr. Glass had killed in his time: shrivelled and numb.

'Oh, come on, nit,' Gus said, shaking Paul's gloom. 'Let's stop worrying and get *Swannie* looking as if someone loves her. She's got to be a credit to us on Saturday, not like one of *Emma*'s poor relations.'

'Do you remember,' Paul said, some little time later when he was touching up the bulwarks with a tin of black paint, '*Swannie* is supposed to be an unlucky boat?'

Gus flung him a withering look from the deck. 'For Pete's sake, Paul, as if we haven't got enough to worry about . . .'

On Saturday morning at eight Gus called for Paul. He found Mrs. Fairfax in the kitchen, putting together Paul's food, while Paul hung over her, saying, 'Honestly, Mum, I could ring him up before I go. That would be all right, surely?'

'Certainly not,' Mrs. Fairfax said firmly. 'It would be most unseemly. Just as if we can't wait to hear all in good time. Anyway, he's probably still in bed.'

Gus grinned, guessing what it was all about. Mrs. Fairfax said to him, 'Paul wants to ring up Mr. Frost to find out what the planners decided yesterday.'

Mr. Frost was the chairman of the Parish Council. 'I bet old Frosty won't know anyway,' Gus said. 'He's always saying nobody bothers to tell him anything.'

'Yes, that's quite true,' Paul's mother said. She handed Paul a bag with his provisions in. 'There, get along now, and stop worrying about it. It'll keep, whether it's yes or no, and you'll want all your wits for the race. I presume I'll see you tomorrow some time?'

'Yes,' Gus said.

'Be sensible, then. And good luck.'

'Good-bye.' Paul kissed his mother absent-mindedly and followed Gus outside. The sun was shining and high white clouds sailed over the marshes. He felt slightly sick.

'It's blowing an easterly,' Gus said. 'What lousy luck, after westerlies all the week. It's going to be a dead-beat all the way to the Bench Head. All right for coming home, but that's not much consolation.' He sent a doubtful glance in Paul's direction. 'I've got to work tomorrow. I thought you could bring her home.'

Paul said, 'Oh, did you?' but not as if his mind was really

on the subject, and Gus decided to let the idea sink in gradually. He would pursue it later. Paul got his bicycle out of the barn. The start of the race was well up the river, off Osea Island, and they had sailed *Swannie* up there earlier in the week and left her on her anchor. Gus felt excited, and pleased because the question of his having to go to work had not been raised. He had to go on Sunday, but Sunday did not matter. He had nothing on his mind to detract from the race. Only Paul. He grinned to himself.

'What if we win, eh?' He got on his bike and shot out of the farmyard. Paul could sense his exhilaration as he followed close behind. He noticed for the first time that Gus's leather jacket had a swan picked out in silver studs on the back. He felt enormously touched, and had a sudden inclination to shout to Gus, 'You can have *Swannie*, if you like.' But Gus wouldn't have heard him, and Paul thought that his father might be rather annoyed if he gave her away, so he said nothing. But he thought she should belong to Gus. He himself cared as little for her as for his clothes or his food or bed, or anything else that was wished on him and taken for granted. All he could think about was Birdsmarsh.

Swannie lay off the beach at Stone, beside the immaculate *Phoebe*. They left their bikes in a friend's shed and begged a lift out to *Swannie* from a passing dinghy. Their own dinghy was to be left behind. It was awkward on deck, and would lose them time if they towed it. Looking at *Swannie* from the dinghy, Paul had to admit that she looked quite smart with her fresh paint and neatly coiled halyards: nothing like the muddy old hulk that had lain for so long in the saltings.

Sydney was up on *Phoebe*'s deck, waving. 'Any news, Paul?' he bellowed, and Paul had to shout back:

'Not yet.'

Once aboard, there was no more time to worry and dream. Gus's enthusiasm was infectious, and Paul, for the first time, began to think quite seriously about the race. What, indeed, if they did win? The idea was quite pleasant. It was time something came out right for them. In company with *Phoebe* they sailed up to the starting-line off Osea pier, where half a dozen more smacks lay at anchor off the island's shingly beach.

With an hour to go to high water, the river off Osea looked deceptively wide. The well-wooded island forming the northern shore was large enough to look indistinguishable from the mainland itself, and on the southern side the wide mouth of Lawling Creek was flooded, its acres of mud shoals hidden from view. Boats and gulls had the landscape to themselves; tanned sails beat easily backwards and forwards across the deep channel, marking time till the start, and the skippers jeered at one another and the gulls jeered back, floating high on the wind above the white topmasts. Paul remembered again that he liked sailing after all, and he was proud of *Swannie*, even if Gus had done all the work. He liked the tension that sparked the smacks' courses, the short, rapid tacks that wove them incredibly, cheerfully clear of bowsprits and counters; the wakes that curved and rippled and were broken by the tide. Spectator boats were gathering, too, and a committee boat, with a row of flags fluttering gaudily from stem to stern, motored down amongst

the mêlée and anchored in her prescribed berth opposite the pier. By the time the ten-minute gun went off there were nine smacks warily jilling for position, and Paul was realizing that he didn't know much about anything, about racing rules, or the course . . .

'Is it just the first home in Brightlingsea? Straight there, I mean?'

'Bench Head buoy to port. That's all,' Gus said briefly. He was occupied with not hitting anybody.

Paul visualized their progress. He had covered most of the ground often enough in the past. It was about thirteen miles from Osea to Brightlingsea, half of them due east down the river as far as Birdsmarsh, where the southern shore bent away and a boat could be considered at sea. Then four miles to the

Bench Head buoy which marked the deep channel north into the River Colne. Round the Bench Head and into the last leg, northwards into the mouth of the Colne to Brightlingsea, which lay in a creek on the eastern bank.

'We'll only have the wind fair from the Bench Head,' Gus said. 'Dead-beat all the way, nearly.'

The wind was steady, a perfect sailing wind, save that it was in the wrong direction. There was another gunshot, which sent the gulls wheeling in alarm.

'Five minutes.'

The tide was slack, and the smacks were all making short tacks just above the line. The vital area of water was a shifting gavotte of weaving sails; Paul was not envious of Gus, keeping *Swannie* where he wanted her without ramming somebody else, and he stood anxiously at the sheets, peering nervously at the swooping bowsprits and hoping fervently that he was going to rise to the occasion. Gus was in no state to suffer fools.

'There she goes!'

Paul saw the faint puff of smoke from the gun before he heard the explosion. *Swannie* was away on her first tack, and Gus's eyes were gleaming.

'Not bad, eh?'

Paul was glad the horrid jockeying was over and that all the boats were now going in the same direction. It looked far less dangerous. Gus seemed pleased with his start, and Paul settled himself on the hatch cover with a feeling of relief. There were two smacks a few lengths ahead of them, three across the river in more or less the same position, and three definitely astern. The ones astern gave him a feeling of superiority already.

'Now we'll find out what *Swannie* can do,' Gus said.

She was butting cheerfully across the river on the heels of a smack called *Falcon*, her patched sails sheeted in hard. Paul watched carefully to see if they were catching up, and could not conceal his excitement.

'We're making on her, Gus!'

'And we're pointing up closer,' Gus said, grinning. 'Ho, we're away, Paul, my lad! Keep your fingers crossed!'

The little fleet of smacks beat doggedly down the river, only gradually spreading out as ability and tactics made their mark.

Swannie passed *Falcon* and two other smacks; *Phoebe* crept up and passed *Swannie*, and by the time they were passing Birdsmarsh they were lying third behind *Phoebe* and *Provident*, a big working smack with a professional skipper.

'And we'll be lucky to pass him,' Gus observed. 'But I don't see why we shouldn't do for old Sydney! He only passed us because we didn't go about soon enough and got out of the tide. Come on, old *Swannie* girl!'

Paul scarcely spared a glance for the familiar sea-wall slipping past as *Swansong* went about off the Birdsmarsh shore. *Phoebe* was on the opposite tack, making out from the Mersea shore, but Gus had already decided that they could point up higher into the wind than *Phoebe*, and would catch her on the next tack. But he had reckoned without Sydney's pride. Sydney's handling of *Phoebe* showed up Gus's comparative inexperience; for all that *Swannie* had the faster hull, she did not close the gap quickly enough to please Gus.

'We will beat him, though, the old buzzard,' he muttered. 'I reckon we'll have him pipped by the time we make the Bench Head.'

There were no boats close enough to worry about behind, and *Provident* was far enough ahead to come into the same category. *Swannie*'s race was with *Phoebe*. Paul could see the Bench Head when he put his glasses on, about a mile beyond a green wreck buoy that at first he had mistaken for the vital mark. He was frightened of missing anything now, and his enthusiasm matched Gus's own. He wanted Sydney to sweat, too.

Gus was working out his strategy to round the Bench Head buoy without wasting any ground. His eyes went from *Phoebe* to the buoy, to his sails and back to *Phoebe*. They crossed tacks, and waved. *Phoebe* was ahead of *Swannie* by the length of a bowsprit, but Gus watched her go away from them savagely.

'We'll be ahead of them next tack. You watch. We'll wave backwards.'

He was right. *Swannie* on the starboard tack had right of way and Sydney had to luff up a fraction to avoid a collision. The two boys danced on the deck, and Sydney waved his fists at them. Gus was beside himself with excitement. His eyes were bright with scorn.

'We'll show him! Poor old Sydney! I bet he's weeping to himself out there!'

'He's laughing,' Paul said. 'He doesn't mind.'

'I do,' said Gus.

Rounding the buoy now occupied his full attention. He judged his distances carefully and went about well off shore for what he estimated would be the last beat out.

'This should just do it. We'll round it by the skin of our teeth.'

Close-hauled, *Swannie* ate up into the wind towards the tall buoy. *Phoebe* had put a quick tack in behind them and was now on their tail, some twenty yards behind.

'Gus, look!'

Paul straightened up suddenly and pointed. 'The seam in the jib's splitting. You can see the sky through it.'

Gus swore violently. 'Get the glue and a bit of sailcloth. It's in the locker over the starboard bunk. We'll bang a patch on. Quick!'

Paul ran. He jumped down into the hold, over Chris's lumbersome suitcase and into the cabin to root in the locker. If the split tore any more, the race would be as good as over for them.

'Here you are!'

'Look, you do it!' Gus was torn by the will to do it himself and the necessity for being in charge to make sure *Swannie* made the buoy. If she freed off too much they would have to put another tack in, and *Phoebe* would catch them up. He watched Paul anxiously. The tear was fairly high up. It meant stepping out on to the bowsprit and more or less leaning on the sail to slap the patch on. The glue, designed to hold lumps of carpet together, was good enough for such emergency measures—if only Paul could reach. As *Swannie* pitched into the swell, Paul staggered and reached out to clutch the forestay. Gus's heart lurched with him. Paul had no confidence moving about the boat when she was in motion. He hadn't done enough of it.

'Come and take the tiller!' Gus bawled. 'I'll do it.'

Paul came back aft, his face puckered with worry.

'Keep your eye on that ruddy buoy and don't miss it, whatever you do. She'll only just make it as it is. I'll be as quick as I can.'

'Oh, God!' Paul breathed to himself. This was the last thing he had wanted to happen—to be in charge at such a vital moment. His hand clutched the tiller in an agony. He had tried close-hauled sailing before. If he didn't free off too much, he put the boat too much up into the wind and stopped her dead. If he did that now, *Phoebe* would charge past. Already he wasn't sure that he wasn't pinching her too much. But there was no room to free off. The tide was carrying *Swannie* down towards the buoy, but to round it she still had to make out some yards to windward. Paul could feel the sweat running down his face. He was so hot with doubt he felt as if he were on fire. A glance forward showed him Gus poised, spread-eagled, against the straining jib, reaching up for the fatal sliver of white sky that showed through it. It was no time to tell Gus he couldn't manage. And yet . . . He looked at the buoy. It was twenty yards away and he knew he was going to hit it. It was about six feet high, a straining cone of iron with a rim of white foam about its neck. In all the wide sea ahead of them, the buoy was drawing *Swannie* like a magnet. Paul pushed the tiller over to force *Swannie* round the buoy, but she lost the wind, and the jib which Gus was clinging to caved in and flogged with a crack like a whip. Gus gave a shout. Paul didn't know what he said, but it sounded furious. He pulled the tiller the other way and *Swannie* started to sail again. She waltzed towards the buoy, bent on suicide.

'*Swannie!*' Paul was almost in tears. He looked to Gus for help, but couldn't see him for the mast. The buoy loomed up on the bowsprit end and Paul heaved the tiller over in desperation.

'Paul!' Gus screamed. He was flinging himself down the deck, his face screwed up and red with fury.

'What are you doing? We've got to round it, you fool! Oh God, we've missed it! Paul, are you mad?'

He flung himself on the tiller and hauled *Swannie* up into the wind to go about. She had cleared the buoy, but on the wrong side.

'To port, I said!' Gus was nearly sobbing. 'Bench Head to port! Oh, Paul, you're mad!'

Swannie was going about reluctantly, the tide holding her up. *Phoebe* was bearing down on the buoy with plenty in hand, and went round it on the right side while *Swannie* was still getting way on her new tack. They could hear Sydney shouting in triumph.

'It was that or hit it!' Paul said furiously.

'Well, why didn't you go about while you still could?' Gus hissed back. 'You know that much, don't you?'

'No, I don't,' Paul spat. 'You said she would make it.'

'Oh, for God's sake, it's finished. Look at *Phoebe*. We'll never catch her now. Oh, the blasted buoy!' Gus put *Swannie* about again, scraping her round the buoy with inches to spare. The anger had died out of his face, leaving it white with disappointment. As Paul mechanically freed the sheets for the reach into the Colne, he stood mutely, feet squarely planted, his calloused fingers clutching the tiller as if they would wrench it off its pintles, watching *Phoebe* turning a smooth wake ahead of him. His eyes were black. Paul thought he looked like his father when he was drunk.

'What about the jib?' Paul said miserably.

'Oh, what about it?' Gus said. 'It doesn't matter. I stuck a patch on. It should hold.'

He sounded as if he were choking. Paul's enthusiasm had died. He felt the old familiar self-disgust taking charge, the old loathing for stupid sailing, the old, old feeling of inadequacy like a lump of lead in his stomach. He stood beside Gus, watching *Phoebe*, and neither of them said a word. *Phoebe* was dancing over the water, flicking up a wake to lead *Swannie* in. Nothing could gain those last yards now; all three of them knew it. Sydney turned round and waved triumphantly, and Gus growled, and muttered something. Paul was tired of trying to explain his failures. He said nothing.

Swannie was third over the line.

Two days before the Saturday of the race Chris was sitting with Proctor by the side of a small lake near Mittenwald, eating cherries and spitting the stones into the water. They sank, spinning slowly, to the clear bottom, and became pebbles, sending up one or two bubbles of protest before settling in their new role. The bubbles reminded Chris yet again of the leaks in his suit. He finished the cherries and lay on his back amongst the

wild flowers. Out of the corner of his eye he could see the spire of the Wettersteinspitze hanging in a hot, gauzy sky, unreal as a backcloth. They had set off to climb it, but, their true natures asserting themselves, they had given up by the lake and had a swim instead. Chris had forgotten what it was like to swim without his suit on. Now the holiday was nearly over he couldn't stop thinking about his suit.

'I just can't understand it,' he said.

He had said it so many times before that Proctor knew what he was talking about even without any introductory preamble.

'What did you do to it, by the way?' he said idly. 'I reckon the whole thing needs remaking now.'

'So do I. It's almost as if the stuff's become porous in places. I just stuck patches over it, like doing a bike, but it won't do. Not if I'm ever to do this twenty-four hour stint. But it just doesn't make sense. There's no reason for it to have deteriorated like that.'

'Sabotage,' suggested Proctor airily. 'A devilish potion administered by persons unknown. A crafty rub with a bit of sandpaper perhaps.'

'Well, I can't think of anything else.'

'There you are then.'

Chris lay on his back without speaking for a long time. Proctor thought he had gone to sleep. Then, suddenly, he sat up.

'I'm going home,' he said.

'On Saturday,' said Proctor comfortably. 'Yes.'

'No. I'm going now,' Chris said. 'This instant.' He stood up and lifted his rucksack on to his shoulder.

Proctor sat up and looked at him.

'I'm a fool,' Chris said, 'to be lying on the side of a mountain like this, when there are so many things to be done. I must be mad. What you said—sabotage. There is no other reason, scientific or otherwise. And I—just lying here in the grass. It's crazy. I can catch a plane tonight.'

Proctor lay down again. 'Yes,' he said. 'You're crazy.'

Chris was already walking back down the track, hitching his rucksack comfortable on his back.

'Good-bye,' he called over his shoulder.

'Cheerio,' said Proctor.

'Look, you can do it easily,' Gus said to Paul. 'I wouldn't suggest it, would I, unless it was so easy a child could do it?'

The uncomplimentary way in which Gus formed his question did not pass Paul by. He bit his lip and scuffled a stone into the gutter with his toe. They were walking down one of the interminable backstreets of Brightlingsea, looking for the place where the prize-giving was supposed to be taking place, and not caring very much whether they found it or not. Neither of them was feeling like a good, smiling prize-winner, for the mistake at the Bench Head had caused too much rancour, and the fact that they were third meant nothing to Gus in light of such shocking incompetence. They had scarcely spoken to each other since the incident, and both knew that the ill feeling had gone too far to mend in a hurry. They had had rows like this before, and knew that the day was doomed. Gus wanted to go home and forget it all, and had told Paul that he must bring *Swannie* home on his own the following day.

'*Phoebe*'ll be going back, too. You can sail in company. The wind's easterly, and the engine's working all right if you need it, so I don't know what you're worrying about. You don't think I'd *rather* work, do you? Blame Reg, if you want to blame someone.'

Paul said nothing. He walked along behind Gus, his shoulders hunched and his hands in his pockets. The day had gone sour on them with a vengeance. Now that it was over he wanted to forget it. It didn't help to dwell on that fatal hen-like panic of his that was for ever betraying him, but Gus would not let the matter lie. He was in his sarcastic, heaven-help-me mood, scowling at the pavement. Paul wished he were at home.

'Oh, Lord, I'd forgotten . . .' he muttered.

They would know now, at home, what was going to happen to Birdsmarsh. Paul could not believe that he hadn't given it a thought all day.

'I must phone home,' he said.

'What for?'

'Oh, for heaven's sake . . .'

Paul pressed along towards the main street, looking for a telephone box. Gus was wishing that they hadn't even come third, then they wouldn't have to go to the prize-giving at all.

'I'll walk on,' he growled at Paul, when he dashed off towards a kiosk. There was a woman inside it, chatting hard, and Paul leaned against the wall, clinking his pennies, watching Gus stalking away down the road. The day was a ruin. What if this phone call were to clinch it, telling him that the scheme had been passed?

'If I ring up, that's what they'll tell me,' he thought. Nothing could go right any more. Some days were like that. Better not to give them a chance. The longer he stood waiting the less Paul wanted to know about Birdsmarsh, because he thought he couldn't take any more for a bit. Not and have Gus ask, and see his eyes light up. The mental vision sent a quiver of self-pity through Paul.

'I can face it tomorrow,' he thought. 'When I've got *Swannie* home all right. I won't find out today.'

He dropped the pennies back into his pocket and walked off after Gus, feeling as if a great weight had been lifted from his shoulders.

'Well?' Gus, not wanting to talk to him, could not conceal his eagerness to hear the news.

'No answer. They must be out,' Paul said.

'Celebrating,' Gus said.

The prize-giving softened their mood a little. Only Sydney had witnessed the fatal mistake; everyone else congratulated them on coming third. They were an embarrassment to the committee, as the celebrations were being held in licensed premises and they were both under age, so nobody thought it strange when they slipped away early. They went back to the harbour, not talking much, but not quite so badly disposed towards each other.

'We never asked Sydney what time he was leaving,' Gus said.

'It doesn't matter,' Paul said, mellowed.

'Are you going to ring home again?'

'It can wait until tomorrow. It's waited long enough.'

It was going dusk and the sky was red over the Colne, the wind gone. Gus stood on the hard, considering.

'It'll be best if we take *Swannie* out of here and leave her on the other side of the river, just in the Pyefleet. It'll make it easier for you to get going in the morning—plenty of sea-room, a straight run out on the last of the ebb. You don't want to have to take her out of the moorings here on your own, especially near low water.'

'No.' The Brightlingsea moorings were cramped and the deep channel was tortuous and narrow. Paul did not want his task complicated. On the other side of the Colne mouth, off the Mersea shore, there was plenty of sea-room for him to play with, and no boats to hit if he bungled things.

'It'll just be a matter of heaving up the anchor. The tide will take her down and you can get the sails up at your leisure. Or motor, if you'd rather. You time your tides right and the old motor will take you all the way to Birdsmarsh, no trouble. You've nothing to worry about at all.'

Paul wasn't worrying any more. He felt that some things

were out of his hands, and this was one of them. Like Birdsmarsh. He had no alternative but to bring *Swannie* home on his own. If he said he wouldn't, he would never be able to speak to Gus again.

The harbour-master gave them a lift out to *Swannie*, and they motored her out of the harbour and across the dusking mouth of the river to the opposite shore. Gus dropped the anchor so that she lay out of the channel. She swung on the making tide, and lay motionless on the still water. Only the tide chuckled against the chain; there was not a breath of wind.

'There,' Gus said to Paul. 'You're fine here for the morning.' He fetched the alarm-clock, and set the alarm with great care. 'High water will be at one in the morning. If I set it for six, that will give you the last hour of the ebb to get out to the Bench Head. Then you'll have the whole of the flood to take you up to Birdsmarsh. You'll be home for lunch. I can tell you, I'd rather be doing it with you than working on those old lorries.'

'Hm.'

A man in an outboard dinghy was coming up the river, going home from a fishing trip, and Gus gave him a hail to see if he could get a lift ashore. The dinghy clattered up and a shouted conversation ensued over the racket of the engine, then Gus was hastily gathering his gear together, and scrambling down over the counter.

'You'll be all right,' he said to Paul.

Paul watched the dinghy head off towards the shore. He did not envy Gus his journey home. The shore where he was landing was miles from anywhere, and the journey ahead of him much longer than the same journey by sea. Paul, suddenly, felt a pang of sympathy for Gus, not just for the journey, but for everything that he had to put up with—his father and his job and having no money and no boat, and having his race ruined by a fool. The dinghy was buzzing over the still water and Gus was just a black speck in the dusk. Paul wanted to shout across to him, 'I'm sorry!' but he knew that Gus wouldn't hear him. It was too late for being sorry. He should have said it earlier, when Gus was fixing the alarm-clock.

'I do everything wrong,' he thought. He felt lonely and odd by himself on *Swannie*, and knew that if he let himself, he could be scared. The night was very still and fine, the sky a rash of stars, the water losing the last reflected light of the vanished sun and darkening perceptibly. When the outboard faded away up the river the only sound was the swilling of the tide under *Swannie*'s counter, strong and persistent. Paul looked towards Mersea, and saw in his mind's eye Birdsmarsh beyond, the line of the shingle beach and the flat silhouette of the sea-wall, broken by a solitary heron.

'Now,' he thought, 'it's all decided. This might be the last night that I can think of it like that.' But he was glad he hadn't telephoned.

'It's better not to know,' he thought. 'It can't be good news. Nothing goes right now.'

Another night to add to the weeks and weeks that he had thought of nothing but Birdsmarsh made no difference at all. He went below and slept.

10

THE UNLUCKY BOAT

Whether the alarm-clock ever went off or not, Paul never knew. He only knew that when he woke up it was half past nine. The clock stood on the stove and its bland face stared at him, and he stared back, and said, 'Oh, God, I've done it again. I've missed my tide.'

He lay for another minute, looking up at the white deck beams, his heart like lead inside him. He could not face Gus again with another mistake, yet it was made before he had started, made in literal unconsciousness. He had missed the tide.

'I've got the motor,' he thought, 'and a fair wind with any luck. It's not completely hopeless.'

He scrambled out of the bunk and went to the companion-way, not daring to hope that the weather might be in his favour. A still, hazy sunlight met his eyes, a meek summer warmth that raised his spirits immediately. Climbing out on deck, he saw the water calm as a pond, the sky cloudless. It was the sort of day that even he was prepared to go to sea on, balmy and sweet, a soft haze promising real heat. He immediately felt better.

'If our old engine can't beat the tide out to the Bench Head, it's not worth its salt,' he thought. 'Then I should get at least a couple of hours' fair tide up the coast. Enough, probably, to see me home.'

What little wind there was had gone round, perversely, and was now westerly, in his favour only for the first leg of the journey. Paul stretched thoughtfully, and looked round, considering what he had to do. He was worried about getting started, up-anchoring and handling the old motor, but once he was under way, he thought, his difficulties would be over. He could get his breakfast at leisure while *Swannie* chunted out to sea. It would be best to waste no time in getting under way, to make the most of what tide would be left to him to get back along the coast.

Feeling very responsible, and sticky with nerves, Paul got dressed and approached the engine down in the afterhold. He had learned how to prime and start it, and now went about the task with great care, squirting a jet of petrol out of Gus's patent squeezy bottle into the cylinder, biting his lip with concentration. Two desperate flings of the fly-wheel produced only unenthusiastic coughs, and he felt the sweat sticking to his back.

'Gus can't milk cows,' he said to himself, and put another squirt of petrol into the cylinder.

This time his assault on the fly-wheel produced a succession of heartening explosions. He opened the throttle, remembering to make sure that the engine was out of gear, and was thrilled by the familiar, frame-quivering racket of *Swannie*'s engine in full throat. He sat back on his heels and wiped his forehead with the back of his hand, leaving a streak of black grease across it. The first difficulty, he congratulated himself, was overcome.

When he was sure that the engine wasn't going to be temperamental he throttled it down and went up on deck to get the anchor in. *Swannie* had a winch, a fairly straightforward piece of machinery which he couldn't see would defeat him. But the strength of the tide made the job a hot and long-drawn-out affair. Twice he went back aft and put the engine in gear to motor up over the chain, but each time the gear lever slipped back into neutral and the smack fell back again. He remembered that Gus wedged the lever with a bit of wood, but the vital accessory seemed to be missing. Eventually he found an old apple-box in the hold which did the job all right, but by the time he had got the anchor in at last and was heading down the river he found it was more than half an hour since he had first gone up on deck.

'Come on, old *Swannie*. Do your best,' he muttered.

His pleasure at getting under way without too much trouble

was tempered by the magnitude of the initial mistake. Although when he looked at the water *Swannie* seemed to be rushing along at a heartening speed, when he looked at the shore he saw that, in fact, for all the splendid clatter of her machinery, she was only crawling along, her effort dissipated by the force of the tide against her. The wind was infinitesimal, not worth getting up sail for, and the heat-haze made the water look as if it were steaming. Three dinghies across the river seemed to hang against a backcloth of misty shingle, their sails useless, the tide carrying them back. No other sails were to be seen. In fact, visibility was poor, and Paul couldn't see the Bench Head buoy that he was aiming for, even through the binoculars.

'I ought to get the chart out,' he thought, 'and lay a course.' Then he thought, 'But it will clear soon. It's bound to.'

For a fleeting moment he wondered whether it would be wiser to put back. But the thought of going home and telling Gus what had happened quenched the idea as soon as it came into his head.

'At least I should get an hour or two of tide with me as soon as I get out.'

But the getting out took longer than he would have believed possible. The tide, flooding along the coast towards Birdsmarsh, was also flooding into the mouth of the Colne, and until he had cleared the river mouth at the Bench Head buoy, he would not get advantage of its force under his keel. At one o'clock it was due to turn again.

'I shall just about get there as it turns,' he thought gloomily.

He groaned under his breath. 'All I want now,' he thought bitterly, 'is to know that Mr. Glass has got the go-ahead to build, and that's it. Everything—everything in the world that can possibly go wrong for me, happens.'

But Birdsmarsh seemed very far away just at that moment. He glanced at his compass. He had no alternative now but to lay a course, for he could no longer see the shore. But the sun was shining; the mist was a veil filled with sunlight. But opaque, nevertheless. Paul began to feel worried. He thought, in spite of Gus, that it might be wiser to go back.

'I'll give it another ten minutes,' he thought. 'If I see the buoy, I'll be all right.'

He knew that weather conditions could change very quickly at sea, and that if he were to turn back the mist would roll away and a fair breeze would spring up out of the sparkling sky, and he would be back in the Colne, speechless with disappointment.

'It's bound to happen,' he thought.

He remembered that *Swannie* was an unlucky boat, and smiled sadly. Was it *Swannie* or her owners? The boat only did what she was asked, after all, to the best of her ability. The mistakes were not hers.

'Poor old *Swannie*,' he said. But he was thinking of himself.

Out of the mist ahead of him a dark shape loomed. His heart missed a beat. At first he thought it was a ship bearing down on him, but the binoculars showed him the blessed silhouette of a black conical buoy. After a few minutes he could even read the name painted on its side, Bench Head. Even a moron like himself could make no mistake about it. Paul's heart soared. All his doubts and guilt complexes fell away.

'Good old *Swannie*! We've made it! We'll really start shifting now! And if the tide turns before we're home, we can manage. We can stem it, or chuck the anchor out if necessary.'

He checked his new course on the chart and heaved the tiller over, feeling like a master mariner. Confidence flooded his very bones. He whistled into the mist, and realized that he was very hungry.

'I've had no breakfast yet. No wonder! I'll go and have a ferret round the galley.'

He went and put the kettle on, and got some bread and cheese, and came back to the tiller. He walked down the deck with a conscious sailor's roll, feeling the swell under *Swannie* and watching the strange sun-shot mist moving like smoke all round her. Already the buoy had vanished, but Paul wasn't worried any longer. He knew where he was; and the compass would see him home. Even if the worst happened and he went aground, no damage would be done in this calm weather.

'Things change so quickly,' he thought, remembering his near despair of a few minutes before. 'Perhaps it's an omen for Birdsmarsh. Perhaps everything will go right now.'

He stood by the tiller, watching the compass, until he thought the kettle should have boiled, then he went forward again and down into the cuddy. He reached for the tea-caddy and put a spoonful in the pot, then he stood by the kettle, giving it another moment to make sure the water was boiling. And as he stood there, there was suddenly a rending crash in the bows. It was the noise of iron smashing wood, a sickening tearing of planks

and screeching of splintered wood that brought *Swannie* up dead in her tracks. Paul was flung violently off his feet. It was as if the whole cabin turned upside down. He got a confused glimpse of the kettle and stove going over together, the loose food and crockery on the table hurtling over his head, and the mattresses jolting up in the air above him. He hit the forward bulkhead hard with his left shoulder and landed in a heap on the floor. And even as he sat there, dazed, he heard the sound of water pouring down the side of the boat into the bilges.

'Whatever——'

His mind was numb. It could grasp nothing at all. He staggered to his feet and obeyed his first instinct to get out on deck. He scrambled up the companion-way and out into the light and looked round in amazement. *Swannie*'s engine was still roaring away, the smack apparently continuing on her way as if nothing had happened. But she was peculiarly down by the head. The deck sloped down towards the bows, not gently aft as it usually did, and Paul could still hear the sound of water rushing above the sound of the engine. He turned round again, dizzy and uncomprehending, and saw the high iron shape of a buoy clearing *Swannie*'s stern. It was revolving slowly from the impact, and Paul saw the letters W—R—E—C—K go past and disappear from sight like the credits of a film title, the mistake spelled out before his very eyes. *Swannie* had hit the wreck buoy.

'Wreck!'

Paul looked round in horror. *Swannie*, still motoring away as if nothing had happened, was, in fact, sinking beneath his very feet. The truth was almost too much to grasp. Paul thought he must be dreaming. He went back to the hatch and looked below. Already the floor in the cuddy was completely covered with water. He could see his anorak floating on the surface, and the loaf of bread, soggy and sinking at the foot of the companion-way. There was a current on the water; it swirled excitedly across the floor and was climbing up the sides of the bunks like a lock filling between sluice-gates. The force came from the bows, and Paul guessed there must be a hole up there big enough to ride a bike through.

As his head cleared, the truth began to sink into his brain.

'I've wrecked *Swannie*. She's sinking.' A detached part of his brain wanted to laugh. It couldn't believe it. It must surely be a joke. But as if to clear up any misunderstanding, the cheerful racket of the engine ceased suddenly, engulfed in a mortal choking noise. Paul found that he was shivering. He realized, at last, that he had to do something. He walked down the deck, which was now only a few inches clear of the water. He went to the stern, and saw that there was no dinghy.

'Oh, God.' He'd forgotten.

He looked round. The mist was like mother-of-pearl, shot through with light, but untransparent. It hung like a silk smoke-screen all round his little drama, cutting him off from all human

aid. He was completely alone. Even the wreck buoy had disappeared. The silence was eerie, like part of the conspiracy, along with the mist, to wrap him up and hide him away from any chance of help. The water, no longer rushing, was coming up over the deck in long fingers, like a making tide.

Paul sloshed back to the cabin and saw that the water filled it completely. Something floated beside the companion-way steps, large and buoyant, and Paul recognized the suitcase with Chris's suit in. It was partly lodged under the ladder, and was beginning to go under with all the rest of the debris, but Paul, a light flashing in his paralysed brain, flung himself down and heaved it out. His hands were trembling.

'Oh, you fool!' he breathed. 'It's the only thing! Oh, God, I'll never get into it in time!'

He fumbled with the clasps on the suitcase, terrified that Chris might have locked it. But they gave, and he dragged the suit out. It looked a tangled mass of complication, limp and lifeless, and Paul felt panic mounting in his breast. He was gasping and his hands shook. *Swannie* was full of water, her old timbers saturated, the heavy engine trying to pull her under, but it was as if she fought it, struggling to stop in the daylight and the sun. The water slopped over her bulwarks and ran along her decks, and she quivered and moaned, rolling slightly in the swell. Paul knew that at any moment she would go from under him like a stone. He took a long, slow breath to steady his panic, and forced his hands to work.

'You've got a couple of minutes at the most,' the detached part of his brain said. He opened up all the zippers methodically, and sat down and got his legs into the lower part of the suit. Then he stood up and pulled it up over his arms and round his neck. It was very difficult doing it for oneself, but he remembered doing it all for Chris in *Woodwind*'s cabin, and he found that he remembered all the zips and the buckles very clearly, so that he knew exactly what he had to do. If only there was going to be the time to do it.

He pulled the long zip up the front, and pulled the hood over his head. It was tight, and he felt stifled, and he could feel the panic taking hold again, the gasping feeling in his throat. He made himself breathe very slowly and carefully to stop the panic, while he got out the air canister and fixed the tube that led into the valve on the chest. As he fumbled he could see *Swannie*'s bulwarks going under in front of him. The water was creeping perceptibly up the coamings round the hatches. A few inches more and it would join the water already inside her. And that would be all.

But the suit was rapidly inflating, and Paul, his breath rasping, almost sobbing in his throat, felt the deck heave under his feet. The water was up to his knees now, and the strange currents were beginning to swirl about him. As the water began to pour over the top of the hatch, globs of air and tortured fountains fighting their way up from below were extinguished by the force from above. It was *Swannie*'s final capitulation. Paul felt her sway like a fainting woman, then there was nothing under his feet at all and he was afloat on his back in the middle of a calm, fog-curtained circle of water, with no sign of any other living thing in sight.

11

PAUL ON HIS OWN

Paul's mind was a nightmare confusion of guilt, fear, and astonishment. For the first few minutes he was scarcely conscious of anything but a raving incredulity and a stark physical terror. He lay rigid, locked with horror, and the calm water lapped all round him as if he were a human shore. Then, slowly, it came to him that he was supremely comfortable, cushioned by air on a wide breast of sun-touched water, smooth as silk. The stiff terror gradually abated, and he was conscious of his limbs relaxing, the anguish dying in his lungs. He licked his lips and lifted an arm and let it fall back. It would not go under the surface, even if he pressed it. He could look down without any difficulty and see the whole island of him, black and shining like a basking whale, slipping idly down the swell. It was how he had seen Chris so often, and worried for him, and now it was himself, on his own, the last thing in the world he had ever imagined.

The first shock over, Paul found that his mind was in operation again. He knew that he was quite close to the shore, that the sun was shining and was likely to disperse the mist very shortly, and that he would then see where he was and act accordingly. He thought that, with the suit to support him, he would be able to paddle ashore, or, if not, if the visibility improved a little, he was bound to be picked up by a yacht or one of the steamers that plied into the Colne. The suit was the saving of him. He could tell by the sun which direction the shore was in, and he paddled towards it with the palms of his hands, waiting for the mist to clear.

He felt curiously excited rather than frightened. Not panicky as he had been earlier, but strung-up. There was an element of triumph in beating imminent death by means of Chris's suit, but it was overlaid with an anxiety about making shore. He had to convince himself that he was going to be all right, and to keep himself paddling steadily. If he faced the sun and kept on paddling headfirst, he thought he would be paddling north towards the shore. There was no other way of knowing. He pulled the hood off his ears once or twice and listened for shore sounds, a train, or a dog barking, but there was nothing. But he knew that it wasn't far away.

'What if the suit hadn't been on board?' The thought kept coming into his mind, numbing the imagination. He could not believe that he had been so near drowning. He remembered that there was a fault in the suit that Chris said he had patched up, but the thought did not worry him. It would be good enough to see him to the shore. He kept on paddling, cupping his hands, keeping the sun above his feet and glancing round occasionally to see if there were any clear patches in the fog. But if anything it was denser, and the sun was very indistinct. Slightly discouraged by the fact, he stepped up the rate of his paddling.

It was almost as if he were alone in the whole world. The shore never materialized and after a little while his wrists got tired. He found it hard to judge how long he had been in the water, and he began to think the tide must have turned. Instead of being carried towards the shore, he would now be going away from it, out along the coast. He stopped paddling, and was conscious of being afraid again, not panicky, as at the beginning, but a slow, real fear at the thought of travelling out away from the shore. He tried to stop thinking about it by concentrating on what Gus would say when he learnt what had happened to *Swannie*. A little while ago the worst situation that he had been able to imagine was telling Gus that he had missed his tide and been unable to get *Swannie* home on his own. Now the recollection of that particular anxiety was ludicrous by comparison with what had actually happened. He had sunk *Swannie* irrevocably, and was now in danger of losing his life. The whole lot of his other worries no longer made sense. What made sense now was the fact that the tide had turned.

He stopped paddling and lay for a long time staring up into the fog. He had had time to get used to what had happened and his mind was now clear. It was no use any longer to pretend that anything else mattered at all, save that he should not lose his life.

The gravity of his situation did not, curiously, make him tremble or want to cry or scream. He had never felt more sane in his life. He felt adult, as old as Methuselah, because he had never been able before to view a situation with such clarity, with such strange, serene detachment. The problem was elemental: merely to live. Gus, and Birdsmarsh, and *Swannie*, and his mother and father were all completely superfluous to this thing in his head. It did not even concern them. This was his own situation, of his own making, and there was no one to help him face it.

The afternoon was drawing on. The fog was, if anything, thicker, and the tide was pulling him out to sea. The slight wind that was now blowing was a westerly, if it hadn't changed since the morning, and was therefore speeding him on his way, not checking his outward progress against the tide. Nobody would start worrying about him for some hours yet, not until Gus came home from work, and by the time they decided seriously that something was wrong it would be dark. Paul remembered again that the suit was defective. He turned his head on one side and watched the water lapping at his shoulders and sliding beneath his head. He remembered when Chris was nearly drowned. The water was calm and two pink jellyfish breathed on its surface a yard away—small, scarcely-living things, but more at home in the water than himself.

Gus got home at six in the evening. He felt tired and dirty and fed-up, but coming down the lane into Birdsmarsh soothed him. He could smell the low-water mud in the harbour, and decided to go and see where Paul had put *Swannie* before he called home.

To his surprise, *Swannie* wasn't there. *Phoebe* was on her mooring, snugged up and obviously deserted, and *Woodwind* lay on the mooring behind her, but there was no sign of *Swannie*.

'He must have missed the tide, the fool,' Gus thought. A twinge of anxiety passed through him. He sat on his bike staring out across the harbour, considering the possibilities. The evening was grey with mist, like a premature autumn evening, and he couldn't see Mersea. He could only see about three hundred yards outside the harbour.

'I reckon that bit of mist this morning put him off. He'll have left her and come home by road, the idiot,' he thought.

He decided to call at the farm, and jumped on his bike again.

He felt annoyed at Paul now, for getting him worried, and pedalled recklessly up the drive to Birdsmarsh, bucketing over the pot-holes. He could not help remembering, all too vividly, that Paul had not been at all keen on the idea of bringing *Swannie* back alone, and that he had more or less forced him into it.

He swept into the yard, leaned his bike against the porch and hammered on the back door. Mrs. Fairfax answered it. Before he had time to say anything, she said, 'Oh, good. I was beginning to get worried about you. How did you get on?'

'Why? Isn't Paul back yet?' Gus said.

'No. Isn't he with you, then?'

Gus felt a cold hand settle on his stomach.

'No. I had to go to work today. He was coming back on his own.'

'On the bus, you mean?'

'No. On *Swannie*.' Gus's voice was soft and ashamed. Mrs. Fairfax gave him a startled look.

'You'd better come in, I think,' she said.

Gus went into the warm kitchen. Mrs. Fairfax said, 'What time should he have been back then, Gus?'

'High water was at one—dinner-time,' Gus said. 'He should have come up on that tide. If he had decided not to come, because of the fog, he would have been home by now. Or rung up or something.'

'He hasn't rung up. Chris rang, to say he'll be home tonight, so the phone's working all right. But not Paul.'

Mrs. Fairfax looked at Gus gravely. 'You say that he was bringing *Swannie* back on his own? I didn't know that was the plan. Do you think that was wise?'

Gus looked back at her miserably. He felt himself colouring up, and could find nothing to say. There was no defence. He now knew that it wasn't wise at all. But Mrs. Fairfax smiled suddenly.

'Ah, well. I dare say he's anchored somewhere if he missed the tide. It's quite foggy out. I noticed just now, when I fed the hens. You can't see the sea-wall.'

'It's calm enough,' Gus said. 'Even if he's gone aground, he can't get into trouble, as calm as this.'

It had taken Mrs. Fairfax herself to allay his own anxiety. Now that she had mentioned it, it seemed pretty obvious that in the fog he had gone aground, or anchored to wait for it to lift. But Gus was shocked at the idea of poor old Paul, stuck with *Swannie* in the fog.

'Perhaps we could ring Brightlingsea, just to find out if he did leave,' he said. 'He might have put back when the fog got worse, in which case they might know something. He could be on his way home by bus now, quite easily.'

'Yes, that's an idea.' She fetched the telephone directory and riffled through the pages. 'We're not worried, though, if he asks me?' It was a question.

'Well, not really. In a fog like this, if he's out in it, he's only got to anchor and wait. There's nothing else you can do. And then he can't telephone.' But Gus knew that if Paul had started when the alarm-clock had gone off he should have been home during the morning. The mist hadn't been bad earlier. Gus wasn't really sure now whether he was worried or not. There were so many alternatives.

Mrs. Fairfax dialled and stood waiting, frowning slightly. Gus was relieved that she was a sensible woman. She could have raved at him for Paul's being on *Swannie* alone. He watched her anxiously. She was explaining the situation to Brightlingsea.

'He was anchored in the mouth of the Pyefleet,' Gus said, 'not in Brightlingsea itself. He should have left at six.'

Mrs. Fairfax repeated this information.

Gus heard her say, 'At ten, you say? You're sure?' Then she said to Gus, 'Has *Swannie* got a black hull? All black?'

He nodded. 'She's MN 32,' he said. 'It's on her bows.'

'And you haven't seen her since? She didn't come back?' Mrs. Fairfax was saying. There was a pause and then she said brightly, 'Oh, no. It's all right. He'll be anchored in the fog somewhere. Or gone aground perhaps. Thank you very much.' She put the receiver down, and the bright look that had gone with her voice died out of her face, and she said, 'They think he left at ten this morning. She's not in Brightlingsea now, at any rate. He said she could be back in Pyefleet, though. But he wouldn't know, because of the fog.'

'At ten?' Gus said. 'He'd have missed the tide all right if he left at ten.' His voice was annoyed. Trust Paul, he was thinking. 'They're sure of that, then?'

'He said a black smack left the Pyefleet under engine at ten. He didn't know her name or number.'

'She was the only one there last night. I suppose it must have been her.'

Gus thought of *Phoebe*, snug and safe in the harbour. Sydney, no doubt, had caught his tide. 'Oh, Paul!' he thought. 'You idiot!' He scratched his head, and almost groaned. 'He'll be out there somewhere, waiting for the fog to lift.'

'Oh, dear, it's a worry,' Mrs. Fairfax said. She smiled at Gus, rather bleakly. 'I wouldn't mind if there were someone with him, but he's a bit of an ass about some things.'

'He'll be all right,' Gus said mechanically. There was not much else he could do. 'I suppose I ought to go home,' he said miserably.

'Yes, you must be ready for your supper. I'd better go and tell Paul's father what's going on.'

They walked to the door together. 'I'll come round later, and see if you've heard anything,' Gus said. 'I'll have another look in the harbour, too, just in case.'

'Yes, do that,' Mrs. Fairfax said.

As Gus rode back down the drive he remembered that he hadn't asked her what had been decided about the plans for Birdsmarsh. Paul would be waiting somewhere in the fog, without knowing what was going to happen to Birdsmarsh. He would be sitting there, worrying himself silly. And worrying everyone else silly, too. Gus felt angry with Paul, but more angry with him for giving him this unusual guilt complex than for any other reason. Gus knew that he shouldn't have made him do the trip alone. If anyone was to blame, it was himself. Angry and tired, he went home. His father was up at the pub and his mother was watching the television. She didn't get up, but said over her shoulder, 'Your dinner's in the oven. Don't complain if it's all dried up. You come home at the proper hour and it might be more to your liking. And get yourself washed before you sit down. You're filthy.'

Gus slammed the door to behind him and flung off his jacket and jersey. The table wasn't laid and the kettle was cold. He looked in the oven and saw a plate of dried-up shepherd's pie and shrivelled chips, and a bowl of stiff rice pudding. He put the kettle on and went into the living-room and stood watching the television. There was a packet of cigarettes on the arm of his mother's chair and he took one and lit it. His mother said, 'Buy your own flaming cigarettes. You're earning now, aren't you?' but Gus took no notice. He leaned against the dresser, smoking, waiting for the kettle to boil, watching the television and thinking about Paul. He had a strange feeling that the day was only just starting, instead of being nearly over.

When he had washed and changed and eaten he went back to the harbour, and walked a little way along the sea-wall, just in case he might see *Swannie* anchored off. There was a soft westerly blowing, but the fog had not dispersed.

'He'll be aground somewhere,' Gus thought. 'Silly devil.'

He supposed he ought to go back to the farm as he had promised, although there wasn't much any of them could do but wait. There was a chance, though, that Paul might have gone into Mersea. Then he could have phoned. Gus got on his bike and rode back to Birdsmarsh. Mrs. Fairfax let him in and he was back in the big, homely kitchen. Mr. Fairfax and Chris were at the table, finishing a meal. Chris looked fit, his face very brown, which accentuated his fair hair and blue-grey eyes and made him look startlingly like Paul. But he looked unusually serious, with a puckered line between the eyes. Gus nodded at him, and said to the farmer, 'Good evening, Mr. Fairfax.'

'What's all this about Paul, then?' Mr. Fairfax said, turning round and looking at him over the spectacles he wore for reading the paper. 'Should we be worried? Getting out the lifeboat? You know all about these things. Tell me what you think.'

Gus told him, to the best of his knowledge. Mr. Fairfax listened carefully, grunting assent every now and then.

'It's just a matter of waiting for the fog, then?' he summed it up. 'Nothing really to get het up about?'

'I don't think so,' Gus said.

'Cup of tea?' Mrs. Fairfax offered.

'Thank you.'

'Ah, well.' Mr. Fairfax moved over from the table to his arm-chair with the Sunday paper.

Gus drank his cup of tea, and said, 'I might as well go home then. If it clears, I'll go down to the harbour at high water again.'

'Thank you, Gus,' Mrs. Fairfax said. 'Thank you for calling.' She looked sad, and Gus felt guilty again, that she was thanking him for getting Paul into this mess. He went over to the door and went out into the yard.

'Gus!'

It was Chris. He came across the yard, and Gus turned round and waited for him.

'Look, I don't know if I should mention this to you, but if I don't discuss the business with someone soon I shall start raving.' Chris's eyes gleamed in the dusk. Gus was conscious of a restless anger bottled inside Chris that was quite unlike his normal easy-going manner.

'What do you know about Peter Winnington? You live here. What do people think about him?'

Gus was astounded. Chris's voice had an edge to it that he had never heard before.

'Paul told me that he was a liar,' Chris went on, 'and I told him not to be a fool. I was angry with him. Do you know what was behind Paul's opinion?'

'Paul thought Winnington had gone on board *Swannie* the night after he rescued you, but Winnington denied it. That's why Paul thought he was a liar.' Gus remembered all the other things Paul had said quite recently. About Winnington wanting to murder Chris when they had gone out on the trial. He looked at Chris doubtfully. He didn't know whether to reveal this choice fantasy of Paul's or not.

'What's wrong?' he asked. 'Why are you asking this?'

'I came back early from my holiday,' Chris explained, 'because of something Proctor said. He said the only reason that the suit could possibly have leaked on the last trial was that it had been got at. Sabotaged. I thought that myself, early on, but naturally one rejects melodrama. These things just don't happen. And then I remembered what Paul said about seeing Winnington coming off *Swannie* that night. He must have had a good look at the suit when he was giving me artificial respiration. If he had wanted to study it properly, it would have been easy for him to have gone back to *Swannie* at high water the next night. And before the trial on *Woodwind* the suit was on the yacht all the night before we sailed.'

'But you're not suggesting Winnington has—has——' Gus couldn't even think of the right word.

'I came home from Bavaria, thinking I was a fool, and so was Proctor, to encourage my fancies. I went straight to Dunfort's the rubber firm, to talk to the man there who is head of the marine equipment division—skin-diving suits and such-like—I had met him before, Carter, he's called, a very decent bloke. I decided it was time to see if they were interested in it, to see if I could get some financial help, an advance or something, because I'm absolutely stuck now for money. I just can't do any more on my own. And when I showed him my drawings he pulled a sheaf of papers out of a drawer and said, "It's something like this." And there was my suit, drawn up to the last zip-fastener.'

Gus stared at him. 'Someone else has got in first——'

'But I knew it wasn't a coincidental likeness,' Chris went on. 'The details were all the same—it was *identical*. It was *my* suit. And when I asked where it had come from he told me that six are being made under a private contract for a private individual, from the drawings supplied. Even Carter didn't know any more than that. They have to be delivered to an address in Chelmsford. Chelmsford! I nearly exploded! I asked if he'd seen the bloke responsible for the drawings, and he said a man brought them in. He described him and it fitted Winnington, which by then didn't surprise me in the least.'

'But what does he want six for, if all this is correct?' Gus was flabbergasted.

'All I can think of is that he wants to sell them abroad, illegally, of course. My God, I'm going to call on him tonight and see what's he's got to say about it all——'

Chris's harangue was interrupted by a voice floating out from the kitchen door. 'Chris! Is Gus still there?'

'Yes,' Chris shouted back.

'Tell him to come here, will you? There's someone on the phone.'

Gus had forgotten what he had called at Birdsmarsh for,

after listening to Chris's revelations, and came back to the present with a shock of surprise. Chris said, 'Don't say anything about all this, will you?' and he shook his head. They walked back across the yard and into the kitchen.

As soon as he saw Mrs. Fairfax's face, Gus knew that the shocks were not over. It was white and crumpled, although she wasn't crying. She held the telephone receiver in her hand, and Mr. Fairfax was standing beside her, saying, 'Take it easy. You can't be sure yet.'

'What is it?' Gus said.

Mrs. Fairfax held the receiver down from her face and put her hand over it.

'It's the police,' she said. 'From Mersea. They say some anglers have just come in and reported seeing the top of a mast sticking up off Mersea Flats. At low water, a couple of hours ago. It's painted white and there's a burgee on it, blue with a white prong on it. Would that be *Swannie*?'

Gus felt the blood drain out of his face. There was a silence in the room that quivered. Gus felt Chris's hand come up and rest on his shoulder, gently.

'That's *Swannie*, isn't it?' he said.

Gus nodded. 'But——' His voice wouldn't come. He cleared his throat and started again. 'It's—it's not only *Swannie*. Several smacks have that burgee. It's the Old Gaffers' Association burgee.' Gus thought it was somebody else talking, not himself. Mrs. Fairfax was repeating what he had said on the telephone. There was a long silence again, and then she said, 'There's something else? What is it, then?'

There was another silence, in which they could hear the distant tinny voice on the telephone. They could not hear what it said, and they waited, watching Mrs. Fairfax's face. It quivered once, and then seemed to straighten and go firm, as if it knew that it mustn't show defeat.

She said, 'Yes, yes. I see.' She picked up the pencil that lay near the phone and repeated a number. 'I've got your number, then. And you'll ring me as soon as you know anything. You'll let us know what you're doing? The lifeboat . . . yes . . . I see. Thank you very much.'

She put the telephone down. There was another brief silence, and then she said, 'The reason they rang us, he said, was that the anglers also brought in a suitcase. It was caught up between the shrouds and the mast, as if it had floated up from the deck when the boat sank. It was empty, but it had "Fairfax, Birdsmarsh" pencilled in the lid. There doesn't seem to be much doubt that the boat was *Swannie*, does there?'

She appealed to them, her face stiff with self-control.

'You—you say the suitcase was empty?' Gus's voice still didn't sound like his own. He looked at Chris, and said, 'The *suitcase*, Chris. That means——'

Chris swore, softly and dreadfully.

'He's using the suit,' Gus said wonderingly. 'It must mean that, Chris. If it's empty.'

'But the suit—Winnington——' Chris's face was white.

'But there's a chance!' Gus said. 'If——'

'What are you talking about?' Mr. Fairfax cut in. His voice was harsh. 'What suit?'

Chris and Gus looked at each other.

Chris said, 'In that suitcase there was a life-saving suit, something I've been working on for the last two years. If the suitcase is empty, it means he must have got into it when the boat sank.'

'You mean, he might be all right?'

'He stands a good chance.' Chris's voice shook. Gus remembered Chris saying that he'd done a 'rough job' of repair on the leak. If it hadn't been for the leak, Gus thought, he'd have given Paul a good chance of surviving. But he could remember all too vividly the consequences of the other puncture, when Chris had nearly drowned.

Chris was explaining the situation to his parents. Gus stood back, conscious of the shock taking root in his very bones, the terrible thing for which he was responsible. The knowledge was unbearable. Cold evidence told him that Paul was very likely dead, and yet his mind would not grasp the fact. It shied away, seeing Paul so vividly, unbearably alive, waving good-bye from *Swannie*'s foredeck. 'It *can't* happen,' his mind kept saying. 'Things like this don't happen to me.' But by merely glancing at Mrs. Fairfax's face, he knew that they did.

'Look, we'd better ring back and explain all this to the police,'

Mr. Fairfax was saying. 'It puts rather a different complexion on things. He didn't have a dinghy, but he had this suit, which means he's floating round in it somewhere. With a bit of luck he'll be picked up all right.'

He picked up the phone, rang the number that Mrs. Fairfax had pencilled on the pad, and passed on the information. Chris described the suit in detail, and the policeman told them that he had already been in touch with the honorary secretary of the lifeboat, and that with this further information they were bound to put out immediately.

'When the fog clears, he said, they'll have the helicopter over from Manston,' Chris said, putting down the phone. 'And the lifeboat is going, and all shipping is being told to keep a look-out, so . . .' He shrugged.

'All this machinery is pretty automatic,' Mr. Fairfax said in a flat voice. 'They do a wonderful job.' He cleared his throat and looked at his wife. Gus could not bear to look at their faces. He backed desperately to the door, and said to Chris, 'I'll go. I'll hang around at home.'

Chris came out into the porch with him. 'I'm going to see that swine Winnington. I can't wait to tell him what I think of him. If only I thought that suit was sound, I'd give Paul a hundred per cent chance! And if it kills him, Winnington will be the one to take the blame. The fabric under the arms is rotted away, and only held together with a patch and some rubber solution. I hadn't the heart to tell them that.' He jerked his head towards his parents in the kitchen.

Gus went home on his bike. Chris in his father's Land-Rover overtook him on the main road, driving furiously, but Gus hadn't the inclination to work out what the result of that particular interview was going to be. He could only think of Paul, who hadn't wanted to bring *Swannie* back on his own, floating alone in the infinite loneliness of the dark sea.

12

GUS CALLS THE POLICE

When it grew dark the fog thickened. It was an autumn fog, a white blanket that Paul could feel wrapping him into a darkness that was as thick as death itself. His world extended no farther than his fingers could reach out. It was as black as pitch, obscuring the comfort of flashing buoys and shore lights and the red and green of passing ships, which Paul knew were there, not far beyond his boundaries. But far enough as to be on the moon, for all the help they could give him. The vibrations of far-away fog-horns no longer raised his hopes. They were merely a background for the close lapping of the water that monotonously fretted his ears.

By dusk Paul had passed through a gamut of emotions which seemed to have left his mind squeezed dry. He felt that he had thought of everything that existed at all in the wide world, and there was nothing else left to think of, and no feeling of despair left that he had not exploited and sickened of. Now he lay listening to the fog-horns, blinking the drops of moisture off his eyelashes. The darkness was scarcely any different, whether his eyes were open or shut. He turned his head in every direction, and there was nothing but the black water and the black sky, invisibly joined, and, when he shut his eyes, his black eyelids. And his black conclusions.

All afternoon he had expected to see a ship or a yacht or a buoy or, as the tide ebbed, to find himself on the dried-out sands of the Gunfleet shoal, or the Buxey. But it was as if he had been steered by some malicious hand clear of all help and hope; he had seen nothing in his small circle of visibility. Pulled out by the tide, encouraged by the steady breeze, he now supposed, by the fog-horns, that he was not very far off the shipping lanes into Harwich, but for some time the noises had not been growing any louder, and he remembered that the tide must have turned again. With the breeze blowing him one way and the tide now pulling him the other, he came to the conclusion that he must be at a standstill, neither going towards home nor towards rescue in the shipping lane. In the early hours the tide would turn again and he would once more start heading east. Whether these theories were correct he had no way of knowing. He was only pleased that he was able to keep calm enough to work out any theories at all. There had been a period when it had begun to go dark—when he realized that nobody would start looking for him, because they would think he was merely anchored, waiting for the fog to lift—when he had almost lost his head. He had shouted, and the shouts had started to turn into screams. His small panorama of mist and water, impervious to his desperation, had seemed to close in, like a box. But even then, when he heard his own voice, he was ashamed, and he had tried to stop his noise, but it was as if he had no control over it. He could hear it going on, as if he were someone else, and all the time he was ashamed. But he *had* stopped it; it was the only comfort he had in recalling the incident, when the noise had choked away and he had merely wept. 'Chris wouldn't have screamed. Gus wouldn't have,' he thought. And then, 'But how do I know?' How could one tell what anybody did in a solitude as fast as his? The thousands of square fathoms of the North Sea that lay in wait for him would give no secrets away. Paul had no confidence in his reserves of courage. When it grew dark, and he knew that he was unlikely to be rescued before the next day, he lay making himself very calm, and after a while it was as if he had grown used to the idea. He did not think about how the suit had leaked, or about how it would feel to drown, or even that he was going to drown. He thought about Birdsmarsh and the narrow shingle beach, and how the sea that was under him was the very water that he loved round the boundaries of his farm. So how could it be such a terrible thing now? But if he were to relax the quivering censorship that he was exercising over his mind, he knew indeed that it was a very terrible, innocent thing, the sea, and that his argument was futile. It was the sea-wall that he loved, keeping the sea in its place, and to look at the sea from a bastion so literally concrete was to experience a fine superior sensation, because the sea was powerless to hurt him. He had not felt like that on *Woodwind*.

The time passed and he had no way of knowing how many hours he had been afloat. He was comfortable enough, considering the circumstances; he wasn't cold, but he was ravenously hungry and thirsty. He kept thinking of cups of tea, and taps of water, and cans of fizz. His face was covered with salt, and the salt got inside his mouth and parched his tongue and throat. The sensation that he had early on, that it was all an incredible dream, that it hadn't really happened at all, no longer existed. He knew only too well that it had happened. He knew that he was alone, more dreadfully alone than anyone reasonably had a right to expect in this world, and that he was in very great danger of losing his life. But he no longer felt like screaming about it. Which was the only comfort he had.

Earlier, Chris had known what he was going to say to Winnington, but in the heat of learning how Winnington's skulduggery had put his own brother's life in danger, his plans were forgotten. Knowing the condition of the suit, Chris thought Paul stood very little chance of surviving until morning—even assuming he had got into it safely. For all they knew the smack had gone down like a stone, and Paul might have been only half in the suit. It was more than likely that he was dead already.

The subject of Winnington's treachery had so completely occupied Chris's mind during the last forty-eight hours that nothing could have kept him away from the Research Station any longer. He was prepared to believe that Winnington might have an explanation, but, one way or another, he wanted to know what was behind it all. And Paul's predicament made the interview even more urgent. He peered into the yellow fuzz ahead of him, braking for the drive up to the Research Station. The Land-Rover lurched in a pot-hole and a scared rabbit fled beneath the wheels. Chris put his foot on the accelerator and roared up to the house.

At first he thought there was no one in, but a second knock brought footsteps into the hall, a light went on, and Mr. Warner opened the door. If he was surprised to see Chris, he gave no indication.

'I called round to see if I could have a word with Peter,' Chris said.

He was invited in, and led to a comfortable living-room at the back of the house, where Winnington was reclining in an arm-chair, watching the television.

'Why, Chris! How are you?' Winnington jumped up, smiling,

and held out his hand. Warner turned the television off, and Winnington said, 'What will you drink?'

Chris, surprised at the warmth of his welcome, had a moment's awful doubt about what he had discovered. If Winnington had anything to hide, his conviviality was remarkably convincing. If Chris had not actually seen his plans at Dunfort's, meticulously drawn out and with the specification typed out alongside, he would have been hard put to it to have been influenced by any of Paul's nonsense or Proctor's theorizing. He had to force himself to relive the scene in Carter's office, while he answered Winnington's small talk about his holiday. It was with some effort that he found himself saying, 'Actually, I've come about something rather serious.'

'Nothing wrong, I hope?' Winnington said.

He was sitting in his arm-chair, relaxed, stretched out, elegant as always, rather like (Chris thought) an advertisement for something expensive. His uncle was pouring a drink at the sideboard, his expression showing nothing, which was usual. Chris had a sudden instinct that it was Warner who arranged things in this household, and if there was any truth in the wild story he had come to believe in, it was Warner who was at the bottom of it.

'Well, yes,' he said. 'There are a whole lot of things wrong just at the moment.'

'Oh dear,' Winnington said sympathetically. He sat up. 'I thought your holiday would have done you good and you'd have come home all unwound and unworried. What's happened? Is it work?'

'Yes, it's my exposure suit.' Chris decided not to beat about the bush any longer. 'I called on Mr. Carter at Dunfort's on Friday.'

There was no doubt that this abrupt statement shook Winnington. An expression of uncontrolled alarm crossed his face, which he made an effort to turn into concern.

'But are you ready to approach them yet? I thought you had quite a few problems to iron out?'

Warner turned round with his drink in his hand, and Chris saw him watching him, giving nothing away. Chris intuitively guessed that he was angry with Winnington for revealing, however fleetingly, his surprise.

'I imagine,' Warner said, 'that they've already been experimenting with similar ideas themselves. I don't want to discourage you, of course, but the probability is obvious. Is this what you discovered?'

'Yes,' said Chris. 'How did you know?' He said it ironically, seeing immediately how Warner was trying to stave off a direct accusation.

'I don't know,' Warner said coldly. 'I foresaw this when I first set eyes on your suit, but one does not like to quench young ambition. I am merely suggesting, now, that you have discovered what I guessed you would: that your idea is not original.'

'I think you know what I'm suggesting,' Chris said, suddenly cold with anger. 'That you made drawings of my suit and got Dunfort's to make it up for you!'

'I think you are being exceedingly foolish to talk like that,' Mr. Warner said, in his cold, formal voice. 'What precisely are your grounds for this accusation?'

Chris told him, in detail. He told him that he thought Winnington had made an examination of the suit early on, when he had first become interested in it the day that he had given him artificial respiration on board *Swannie*. Paul had seen him on board *Swannie* the night after the accident happened. He also had good reason to believe that they had tampered with the suit the night before the test on *Woodwind*, and made it porous in places with sandpaper to cause seepage, so that the test had been a failure. This, he believed, was to hold up his approaching Dunfort's, which he would have done immediately if the test had been a success.

Warner listened to the recital without a flicker of emotion disturbing his features, but Winnington listened almost eagerly and, at the end, laughed.

'Really, Chris, you're being ridiculous about this whole thing. After all, why should we want to do this? Why *should* it be us? We've gone out of our way to help you, I would have thought.'

'Yes, I'm very puzzled myself,' Chris said. 'But when Carter described you to me, and said the suits were to go to an address in Chelmsford, I don't see how I could have come to any other conclusion.'

Winnington said, 'That was very indiscreet of Mr. Carter.'

Warner, for the first time, showed a spasm of anger, but Chris knew it was for Winnington's indiscretion, as vital as Mr. Carter's own. His remark was an admission of guilt. Warner drank off his whisky and put the glass down with a sharp click on the polished table.

'Come along to the office,' he said to Chris. 'I've something to show you.'

Chris got up and followed Warner out of the room, with Winnington behind him. He was wondering what defence they were going to make, or what explanation he was going to receive; but when he had gone into the office, and Winnington had shut the door behind them all, he thought he knew then what he should have foreseen when the invitation was issued. The office was a small, bare room, with a row of filing-cabinets along one wall, a large safe and a desk. The window was barred, to keep burglars out. Winnington was leaning against the door, and Warner sat on the corner of the desk and said, not to Chris, but to Winnington, 'It only means going a few days earlier than we intended. We're extremely fortunate, if you look at it in that light.'

Winnington said, 'You mean we must go now?'

'I don't see that we've any alternative,' Warner said sharply, 'since you never seem to learn tact.'

'Oh, Lord,' Winnington said. He scratched his head wearily. 'And what do we do with Chris?'

He looked at Chris without malice. He even smiled slightly.

'You don't do anything with me, if I can help it,' Chris said. He stood with his back to the wall, between the two men. His mind was flooding with self-reproach: fool, fool, *fool*! How stupid could a man get? It was coming to him now and he deserved everything he was going to get, because he had been such a blind, blundering fool. What had he expected, for heaven's sake? An apology? In his stupid indignation he had thrown prudence to the winds. In his impetuosity he was just an idiot child. No wonder Winnington could afford to smile.

Warner was glancing at his watch. 'We only need about twenty-four hours' grace. After that he won't be able to harm us. A good shot of paraldehyde should do the trick.'

'There, you can sleep it off,' Winnington said to Chris, looking relieved.

'I'm not tired,' Chris said, and launched himself at Winnington, head down. His move was so quick that Winnington had no time to move; he received the full force of Chris's tackle in his diaphragm. He let out a surprised grunt and went down heavily, but even as he fell Chris felt rather than saw Warner launch himself off the desk. For an older man he was surprisingly quick. He had a heavy glass pen-tray in his hand and he swung it at Chris's head. Chris was too late to duck fully, and the implement glanced off his temple with sufficient force to send him staggering back amongst the filing-cabinets. As he lost his balance Warner did a neat step-dance and launched himself in pursuit once more, and the two of them went down with a resounding clanging all round them of metal filing-cabinets.

Chris guessed he could have been a match for one of the men on his own, but it was impossible to beat the two of them. Winnington, still gasping, was standing over the two struggling figures on the floor, waiting for the opportune moment to clout Chris once more with the pen-tray which he had picked up. Warner, aware of the intention, shoved Chris away from him.

A wire trayful of papers tipped off a cabinet and rained down, blinding Chris for a fateful moment. He threw up an arm desperately, but heard Winnington's gasping breath close to his face, then felt a stunning blow across his cheek-bone that knocked him sick. He heard his own breath escape in a hurt grunt, and his energy seemed to dissolve. He lifted himself up on one elbow, but hadn't the strength to get any farther.

Warner stepped back, pushing his thin hair back in place.

'Stand over him,' he said to Winnington. 'I'll get the syringe.'

Chris couldn't focus properly. His head was reeling. He heard Warner leave the room, and Winnington saying, 'You are a ruddy fool, Chris,' then Warner was back, muttering and swearing to himself as he fiddled with something at the desk. Chris tried to get up, but Winnington pushed him back. He saw the glint of the needle and felt the stinging jab in his arm. He couldn't believe it.

'That's fixed him,' Warner said to Winnington. 'Now start getting your things together. The sooner we go the better.'

But Chris didn't hear him.

Gus got up as soon as it was light, after a terrible night. He had never before experienced despair or grief or guilt in any real measure, let alone in such an overwhelming tide as this. His head ached abominably. He went to the window and pushed the curtains back, and saw the mist still lying over the marshes, not very thick but still lying. And a soft breeze was still blowing off shore. He could see the mist moving, and parting, and sliding out over the sea-wall, and the pale light of the rising sun diffused through it, soft as the light through the curl of a sea shell.

'It *must* lift when the sun comes up. Or they'll never find him,' he thought.

He went downstairs. It was too early to go to the farm. He put the kettle on and leaned against the draining-board, waiting for it to boil. There was no point in getting up so early, but no point in doing anything else, either. He made a cup of tea, and went outside. It was only three minutes' walk down to the harbour, so he went there and stood on the quay. Immediately he noticed that *Woodwind* was missing.

In his preoccupation with Paul he had forgotten all about

Chris's furious drive down to the Research Station. Seeing *Woodwind*'s empty mooring, his first thought was that she had left to search for Paul.

'Winnington must have had an explanation for Chris,' he decided. 'And when Chris told him what had happened they went off to help search for Paul.'

It seemed pretty obvious. The Land-Rover was parked by the side of the quay.

'I wish I'd known,' he thought angrily. 'Then I could have gone, too.'

Anything would be better than just waiting about. He went heavily back up the street and into his house to look at the time. It was seven o'clock. He decided to go up to the farm, and dragged his bike out of the back shed. He wasn't going to work, that was for sure.

Up at Birdsmarsh, Mr. Fairfax was in the milking-shed, going about his jobs as usual. One look at his face told Gus all he wanted to know.

'No news?'

'No. Only that they're out searching. But in this weather it's pretty hopeless. According to the weather forecast it's not going to clear much today, either.'

They looked at each other bleakly. Then Mr. Fairfax said, 'Did Chris go off with you last night? He seems to have disappeared, too. Pretty inconsiderate of him, in the circumstances.'

'I think he's gone with Mr. Winnington in his yacht, searching. The boat's gone, anyway.'

'He might have let us know.'

'Didn't he ring you?' Gus was surprised.

'No. Not a word.'

Gus stopped and helped the farmer clean up the shed and let the cows back out on to the marshes, then he rode slowly back to the village. He didn't want to see Mrs. Fairfax. He thought it was very odd that Chris hadn't rung up to say what he was doing, and wondered what had happened at the interview last night. Chris had been furious. If he'd been right, that Winnington *had* swindled him over the suit, if Paul had been right all along . . . Gus began to feel slightly alarmed.

'I'll call up there and see if Mr. Warner's around,' Gus thought. 'I can say Mr. Fairfax wants to know what's happened to Chris.'

He pedalled up the road through the swathes of mist. Generally a couple of technicians came to work at the laboratory behind Warner's house, but it was too early yet for them to have arrived. Gus parked his bike and knocked on the door of the house, but nobody answered him.

'Warner must have gone, too,' Gus concluded.

But it seemed very unlikely that he would have gone, too. Winnington perhaps. And even Winnington . . . 'He has to go to work, after all,' Gus thought. 'And they know the lifeboat's gone out. It's not as if there's not a full-scale search laid on already.'

Gus didn't know what to do. He kept remembering that Chris had come all the way home from Bavaria because he thought Winnington was a crook.

'What do you want up here, my lad? Looking for someone?'

Dismounting majestically from a solid, old-fashioned bicycle was a stout woman in a head-scarf and fawn mackintosh. Gus recognized her as a village woman.

'Yes, I want Mr. Warner, but there's no reply.'

'No reply? He didn't tell me he was going out. He does usually, because of the key,' the woman said. Gus remembered that she was called Mrs. Percival, and presumed she was Warner's charwoman.

'We'll see if it's in its hidey-hole,' she said. She had parked her bike, and was looking under a stone in the flower-bed.

'No.' She straightened up. 'Let's try the back door, then,' she suggested.

Gus followed her round to the back, and watched her attack the back door. But it was locked.

'Very odd,' she said. She hammered on it loudly, and called out, 'Mr. Warner! Mr. Warner!'

'He always tells me if he's going out,' she said. 'I come every morning. It's not as if he could have forgotten.'

Gus was thinking, 'If they went out to search for Paul, they wouldn't have been in a great hurry. They'd have remembered the key and things like that. But if there was a row, and something had gone wrong . . .' Gus began to feel distinctly uneasy. Paul had spoken of murder. So far, everything Paul had gloomily prophesied seemed to have come true. And why hadn't Chris rung up? Gus could feel a small panic rising as he stood there, staring at the silent house.

'Do you think there's something wrong?' he asked the woman.

'Wrong? Well, it's odd. He's never done this before. But, of course, if something cropped up, and he forgot the key . . . well, that's it. I might as well go home.' She shrugged.

Gus followed her round the front again. He decided he would go and see Bob Turner, the policeman. Turner would be concerned with the Fairfax family as it was, and could at least take the responsibility. Gus was too worried to leave things as they were, although it was the first time in his life he had ever thought of turning to the police for help. He had had several brushes with Bob Turner in the past, but not in the course of asking for help. It was a complicated tale he had to present: he only hoped Turner would have the patience to listen.

He met Turner on his bicycle, on his way up to the farm. He stopped, and Gus asked if there was any news of Paul, but he could tell the answer before the question was out, by the policeman's manner. Turner was a youngish man, and on good terms with the Fairfax family. For Paul's sake he was now quite sympathetically disposed towards Gus, and listened to his story with pointed interest, leaning on his bike on the grass verge. In fact, he seemed more interested in Winnington's activities than in Chris's disappearance.

'In actual fact, you say now that he has left in his yacht, presumably with Mr. Warner as well?'

'Yes. It looks like it. But what's happened to Chris? If he went with them, he would surely have phoned home first?'

'You'd have thought so.' Turner got on to his bike again. 'We'll go up there and have a look round, shall we? Someone in the laboratory might know what's going on.'

Once more Gus found himself riding slowly up the drive of the Research Station, this time behind Bob Turner's bicycle. The day had already taken on the quality of a dream, or a nightmare, where everything had an unreality. Even the house, standing out square and not very beautiful in the mist, had a sinister, secretative look about it to Gus's eyes. The heavy summer elms dripped moisture in great silent drops all over the concrete paths, and a few leaves had already fallen. Gus had lost all sense of time, and was amazed when Turner said, 'It's gone nine o'clock. Let's try the lab. There should be someone there.'

The laboratory lay behind the garage; it was a small prefabricated building given over to a study of the habits of the local oyster. Two men were sitting on a work-bench laughing at something, and were obviously startled at Turner's sudden appearance in the doorway. They stood up hastily.

'Mr. Warner not about this morning?' Turner asked.

'We haven't seen him yet.'

'He wasn't going anywhere, that you know of?'

'He didn't say anything.'

'Hmm.'

Turner retreated and said to Gus, 'Not much we can do really. I can't enter the house without a warrant.'

'But what if Chris——'

'He's probably on the yacht with them.'

'But——' If he were, Gus knew that Chris was in trouble. It couldn't be otherwise. The feeling of disaster had settled in Gus's bones. 'We can look through the windows, can't we?'

Without waiting for Turner's reply, Gus crossed over the terrace to the back of the house. The french windows of the living-room were curtained, and he could see nothing in there. The kitchen was empty, and tidy. He walked round the side of the house, with Turner anxiously following, to a barred window. and peered through. There were net curtains up, which made it difficult to see anything, but through a slight gap in the centre Gus could see that the room was an office. He could also see that one of the filing-cabinets had fallen over, distributing a pile of papers like snowflakes all over the room.

'Look,' he said to Turner.

'Hmm,' said Turner again.

'That's strange, surely?' said Gus angrily, goaded by Turner's phlegm. 'Surely we can do something?'

Turner scratched his chin. Then, with a surprising ring of

decision in his voice, he said to Gus, 'Yes. We must follow this up. First of all, that means my making a few phone calls. It might take some time. You can hang about here if you like, or come with me. Better come, probably.'

The phone calls took most of the morning, and seemed to involve much sitting about waiting for answers to come back. Gus got the impression that the whole unlikely tale was being relayed to higher realms of the police hierarchy; he also got the impression, for some reason he could not fathom, that the higher realms were taking a whole lot more interest in the case than he had imagined they would. This was evident when, at twelve o'clock, Turner took him back to the Research Station and they were joined by a patrol car with no less than four men in it, two in plain clothes.

This time there was no reticence about breaking into the house. The back door was forced, and shortly afterwards the locked office was broken into, and Chris was carried out into the living-room and laid on the couch.

'It's all right,' one of the plain-clothes men said to Gus. 'He'll be right as rain in a few hours, when he's slept it off.'

'What's wrong with him, then?' Gus asked in a choked voice. The unreality had given way with a vengeance. Gus felt dizzy.

'He's been given a shot to keep him quiet for a bit. It's the modern equivalent of tying a man up and locking him in a wardrobe. Very tidy and painless. We'll have the doctor down to have a look at him all the same. The sooner we can hear what happened here last night the better.'

The other plain-clothes man was already on the telephone. They kept on and on telephoning. To Chelmsford. To London. To Harwich.

Turner looked very pleased with himself. He said to Gus, 'They don't stand a chance of getting away. A Trinity House vessel is going out to pick them up. The lifeboat that's out searching for young Paul has given them a fix on her. Apparently they stopped her a couple of hours back to tell them to keep a look-out for Paul.'

Gus could not understand why it was so important that the Trinity House ship should be going out. It was only a personal row between Chris and Winnington, after all. Chris was not harmed. Gus could not feel interested in all this excitement any more. He did not understand why Winnington and Warner had fled, and why the C.I.D. was involved. He only knew that he daren't go home for dinner, because his parents did not know he wasn't at work. He left the house without anyone noticing and went down to the harbour. He left his bike and started to walk along the sea-wall, on Paul's land. He walked along until he came to *Swannie*'s old mud-berth, the outfall where the stakes were still sticking up out of the saltings, and then he sat on the bank and laid his head on his arms.

'Paul,' he said out loud. 'Oh, Paul!'

There was nothing else he could think of now. He started to cry, looking at the flooding gap in the saltings where *Swannie* used to lie, and the forlorn stakes that would no longer hold her.

13

THE LONG DAY

By the afternoon of the second day Paul knew he was beginning to get light-headed. For hours he had lain watching the sun shining through the mist, waiting for the blue sky to show through the drifting veils of moisture, waiting for a momentary lifting that might show him a horizon. Sometimes the fog cleared to what he thought might be as far as a mile away, but he never saw anything. He dozed uneasily, and when he opened his eyes he saw the sun faintly shining and the mist drifting, and he dozed again, and awoke suddenly, and saw a yacht in the mist. He knew it was *Woodwind* by the number on her sail. It seemed, in that moment, that it could only be *Woodwind*; it seemed right and inevitable that she should be there. He tried to shout, but his voice wouldn't work. The yacht was like a ghost slipping through the mist. She had gone almost before he had forced out a painful croak, and he knew that she had been a mirage, a figment of his wishful thinking.

'She wasn't true,' he thought. 'I'm seeing things.' But the image had been so clear. In the faint breeze on the calm water she had been slipping along like the thoroughbred she was, her white hull reflected, the bow-wave from her stem spreading out like ripples from a swan.

'Perhaps she was looking for me,' he thought. And then, 'But she wasn't there. It was a mirage. Or I dreamed it. You can see things in a dream as vividly as in real life.'

Even so, he tried to shout again, but could raise no more than a croak. His throat felt swollen and burnt, his tongue like felt. He opened his mouth and splashed sea water into it, rinsing it round and spitting it out again, but soon it felt worse than before, and the taste of salt aggravated his dreadful thirst. His whole body was wracked with the thirst. He dozed again, but now he was afraid that these lapses into semi-consciousness were a beginning of the long-drawn-out decline into the ultimate unconsciousness that he had already visualized, and he fought to keep his eyes open, and his brain working. Whether he was frightened now he no longer knew. His emotions were blunted, and he could think of nothing logically. In his mind, over and

over, he could hear the melody from the slow movement of Beethoven's Seventh; it went on and on, as he lifted and slid down the undulations of the sea swell. It had no meaning, only that it fitted in with his sliding and floating and the great depths that lay beneath him, which he could look into when he turned his head, and contemplate with a detached awe. He felt very far away, in time and experience and emotion, to all the things that had ever happened to him before. He felt as if half his life had been spent on the surface of the sea, listening to the melody in his head, and all the things he remembered he had worried about before were as infinitesimal as the grains of sand on the sea-bed. There was only one thing to worry about in the whole world, he thought in a moment of unpleasant clarity, and that was merely not to die. But even the thought of not coming out of this ridiculous thing was as fuzzy as the rest of his thoughts. It was as unreal as the image of *Woodwind*. He felt very tired, and he wanted to go to sleep. It was his only real, conscious thought, that he wanted to go to sleep, and that he mustn't.

At six o'clock in the evening the fog lifted. It dissolved, leaving an evening sea as dark as sapphire, white-flecked here and there with a rising wind from the west, and a sky almost without clouds. The sun soaked up the moisture within an hour; the grass smelled pungently across the fields, wet and hot at the same time. Gus, not daring to face Mrs. Fairfax again, went up to the police house and found Bob Turner in his office, whistling.

He stopped whistling when he saw Gus.

'Come in. Sit down.'

'What's happening? Paul——'

'No. But I've just heard from Clacton. The lifeboat was on its way back, but now the fog's cleared they're staying out till it goes dark. And the helicopter is coming over from Kent. But, Gus——' He hesitated.

'Yes, I know,' Gus said heavily.

'Don't bank on anything.'

'No.'

'As for the other thing, *Woodwind* was picked up by the Trinity House vessel. The Harwich police searched the yacht and found everything they had hoped to find. I can't tell you what it's all about at the moment, but it's a very big case. Warner and Winnington have both been taken into custody. I can tell you, you're responsible for a great deal, stopping me this morning.'

'How's Chris?'

'They're still waiting for him to tell them what happened. He's shown signs of coming round, I think.'

'Do Mr. and Mrs. Fairfax know what's been going on?'

'I went up to see them a short while ago. I told them the story roughly, but I don't think it meant a lot to them. It's only Paul they're worried about at the moment, naturally.'

'When it gets dark, does it mean they'll finish searching for good?'

'I'm not sure, but I think it's pretty likely. It's been a long time, Gus.'

'I know that.' Nobody knew better.

Gus went outside again, and walked down to the saltings to be on his own. Three hours more. It was very warm. The wet mud shone like gold in the sunlight, and the air was full of waders' twitterings and bickerings. To Gus, who had never thought the local landscape particularly beautiful, it was as if he were now seeing it through Paul's eyes. Feathers of pink cloud drifted up above the sinking sun and a sea-gull that hovered there, crying thinly on the wind, was outlined in gold against the spears of light like a painted dove in a Catholic church.

'Oh, Paul, you fool,' Gus whispered. When the sun had gone it wouldn't be beautiful at all.

He waited there, lying in the grass on the hump of the sea-wall, until he saw the first star shining above the first light that appeared on Mersea Island. Then he got up and started to walk home.

Paul saw the first star through the heavy drifts of semi-consciousness, and heard a noise in his head that was neither Beethoven's Seventh Symphony nor a figment of his imagination. He could not guess what it was, but knew that he ought to care. He tried to lift an arm to wave, but his arm felt as if it were made of lead.

The noise was very loud, like a tractor in the sky. Paul forced his eyes open, and saw an ungainly black bird hovering over him. The noise battered him out of his torpor. Two faces were peering at him scarcely ten feet above, grinning, grimacing faces nodding their heads, in the glass front of the helicopter. Paul felt as if something had exploded inside him. He shouted—anything, it made no difference, for it was only a croak drowned by the shattering vibrations that had so suddenly engulfed him, swept away by the down-draught of the rotor-blades that were like a miniature gale blowing. Through the rotors the first star was trembling; the helicopter's greenhouse front was aglow with a rosy reflection from the last light of the sun. Paul realized now, for the first time, that he could see the horizon in every direction. There was no land in sight, only the clattering world of the helicopter black against the glowing sky. It was the loveliest thing Paul had ever seen. He lay there, laughing and waving and shouting soundlessly into its fantastic noise.

Sydney was walking down the village street, and Gus could see that he wouldn't be able to slip into his gate without avoiding him. He advanced with his jaunty step, looking strange in a city suit, without gum boots.

'Gus! I came straight down when I heard the news! What a shock it was, to hear it over the wireless! I didn't know what I could do, but I had to come. I felt responsible, you see, to a large extent——'

Gus shook his head. He was past wanting to speak to Sydney, or anyone, come to that.

'But, thank God, it's all right,' Sydney said. 'I shall only be in the way now, if I go butting in, but if you see Mr. and Mrs. Fairfax, tell them——'

'What do you mean, it's all right?'

'Now that they've found him.'

'They've found him?'

'Yes, didn't you know? Turner told me when I just called in. He'd had the news, and was just on his way out to the farm. A helicopter picked Paul up. He's quite all right, conscious and in good spirits, so the message said. You hadn't heard?'

He peered at Gus in the dusk. Gus said nothing. He was very pale. Sydney put a fatherly arm round his shoulders.

'Come with me. You need a drink, and so do I. If you're under age, it's doctor's orders. What a day you must have spent!' And he steered Gus gently in the direction of the pub.

Later, when he was on his way home, Gus remembered that he had never thought to ask what was going to happen to Birdsmarsh.

14
BIRDSMARSH

Mr. and Mrs. Fairfax drove over to Colchester to see Paul in hospital the same evening. They were astounded to find themselves accosted by an eager group of newspaper reporters and photographers when they got out of the car, and, after the experiences of the last twenty-four hours, felt overwhelmed and bewildered when they at last shook themselves free. 'This way,' said a nurse, and they followed her though a maze of warm, white corridors and up in a lift, and through some swing doors and down another white corridor.

'There's really nothing the matter with him. It's just a safeguard, to keep him overnight. You'll see for yourselves.'

'Oh, Jim,' Mrs. Fairfax said suddenly, clutching her husband's arm. 'You know—I'd forgotten—he—he's bound to ask——'

'Ask what?' The farmer felt embarrassed and out of his element. He hated hospitals and fuss, and Paul had landed him with both.

'About Birdsmarsh, of course.'

Mrs. Fairfax had stopped in her tracks, and the nurse was turning round to see what had happened.

'Well, he's got to know. What can you do about it?' said Mr. Fairfax. He looked at her impatiently, then softened, and said, 'You could do with a spot of bed yourself, by the look of you. Come on, now. Fancy worrying about that, after all you've gone through!'

'In here,' said the nurse.

'Oh, Jim, I wish——'

'A real fraud. Look at him,' said the nurse.

Paul was suntanned against the stiff white linen, and looked sheepish when he saw them. He lifted himself up on one elbow and said, 'I'm sorry——'

'Oh, Paul!'

The first moments of the meeting were confused in Mrs. Fairfax's mind. She never remembered what she said to Paul, only that he said nothing at all, save that he was sorry, and that in a few minutes a doctor and a sister came in, and then two of the more persistent of the newspapermen, and everyone seemed very jolly and talkative. Even Mr. Fairfax stopped looking uncomfortable, and unbent to the reporters, until the doctor said, 'Well, I think we'll leave him to it now.'

'Good-bye, Paul. They say you'll be home tomorrow.'

'Yes.'

'Good-bye. We'll come over and pick you up when they give us the word.'

They backed to the door, and the doctor said, 'I'll just have a word with you before you go.' He went into the corridor with Mr. Fairfax, and Mrs. Fairfax turned to shut the door, but Paul was watching her.

'Mum—come here a minute.'

'What is it?' she said, knowing perfectly well.

He didn't say anything, and she went back to the bed and said, 'It's been passed, but with conditions. It's not so bad as it might be, Paul.'

'They're going to do it?'

'Yes. But they've thrown out the hotel and the swimming-pool. They've said just essential services, a repair shop, a chandler's and what have you. And a car park for five hundred cars. But none of the clap-trap.'

'And Mr. Glass had accepted that? He's going to do it?'

'Yes. He rang us up and told us he was going ahead.'

Paul didn't say anything else. There was no expression in his face. His mother looked at him in despair, almost exasperation, keyed up herself to expect some sort of an outburst. There was a look in his eyes that she could not read, and an unfamiliarity about him that baffled her. She had expected that she would have to comfort him, but now she had the feeling that it was she herself who needed comfort.

'Are you all right now?' she asked. 'I must go.'

'Yes. Quite all right, save that the bed seems to be going up and down all the time.'

'You won't worry—about——'

'No. I knew, really.'

'Good-bye, then.'

Mrs. Fairfax walked out into the corridor with a feeling as if she had gone to visit a dentist, expecting something terrible, and that he had sent her away without doing anything. 'I'm old-fashioned,' she thought. 'Dentists don't hurt any more.' But it didn't explain Paul. The doctor shook her hand; they were away through the white corridors again, following the nurse.

When they were driving home, Mr. Fairfax said, 'That doctor fair flummoxed me. Do you know what he said about Paul?'

'No. What?'

'He said he showed an "extraordinarily mature mental attitude for his age". He was going on about his "stable" character, and the remarkable way he's come out of all that happened. I nearly said, "Who are you talking about? Our Paul?" '

'Well, I must admit I was surprised. When I told him about the plans he just said, "I knew, really". He seemed ever so much older. I was completely baffled.'

'I don't know about his experiences ageing him, they've certainly aged me,' Jim Fairfax said. 'It's nice to think he showed up like that, though.'

'I can't think that he's actually changed. But grown up, possibly. I don't know.' Mrs. Fairfax yawned compulsively. 'He's a difficult character, after Chris.'

'For Pete's sake, what was all that rigmarole about Chris?'

Mr. Fairfax slowed to negotiate a right-angled bend. 'I never did take that in properly.'

'He should be home when we get back. Bob Turner said he'd bring him home when he'd come round. But come round from what I never did gather, except that he'd been in some sort of a rough-house, and that Peter Winnington was involved. But why he had to choose such an inopportune time to go brawling is quite beyond me. I merely satisfied myself that he was in no real trouble and put it out of my head. Enough is enough. I never want to go through a day like this again.'

It was almost midnight when they got home. Chris was lying in an arm-chair looking strangely excited. The kettle was simmering on the Aga, and moths were diving and bumbling round the light. The air was warm through the open windows and the sky was full of stars, as if the thick fog of the night before were a long-ago long-forgotten thing.

Chris got up and started making a pot of tea.

'He's all right, is he?'

'Yes. Amazingly so. He looked no different at all, not even shocked.'

Chris beamed. 'My suit, you see. Thirty-three hours he did. Do you realize that? Better than any mere test could have been. Thirty-three hours, and I dare say he could have doubled it, trebled it, if he'd had some water and food. My word, this is the most fantastic, freakish stroke of luck for me that could ever have been devised.'

'*Christopher!* You brute! You utter brute!' His mother looked at him, dazed and uncomprehending. She saw his eyes dancing in the electric light as he poured out the tea.

'Poor old Mum. Here, have some tea. Yes, I know I'm a brute, but Paul will understand. Believe me, I wouldn't have wished it on him, but he will know what it means to me. It will be in all the newspapers tomorrow—thirty-three hours. Carter knows all about it—he rang me up an hour ago. He wants to see me first thing in the morning.'

'Who's Carter? And why?' Mrs. Fairfax said wearily. 'Oh dear, I don't really understand all this, Chris. I can't take any more in. What happened to you last night?'

'Oh, that! That's yet another story. I shan't trouble you with that now. Paul's responsible for that little lot, too, when you come to think of it. He really sparked things off when he sank that smack.'

'It's no good. I must have a night's sleep before I listen to your ravings. Oh, thank God, I can sleep in peace tonight!'

'It's been a queer old couple of days,' Mr. Fairfax said squarely. 'You can lock up, Chris. Come on, Liz. You're all in.'

'Can I take the car to the station in the morning, Dad?' Chris asked. 'I'm seeing Carter at ten. It'll mean an early start.'

'I shall want it to fetch Paul later. I'll run you there and bring it back.'

'Thanks. That's fine.'

They all went to bed. Paul's mother looked at the stars through the window and hoped Paul was asleep, not thinking about Birdsmarsh. She wondered if they would give him something to make him sleep; then thought perhaps they had, before she had seen him, and his strange inner tranquillity—she could not think of the words to describe how Paul had looked—was due to drugs. There was no way of knowing, until he came home. She slept. When she awoke it was late. Chris had gone. The sun was shining as if nothing had ever come to disturb the farm's timeless routine, slanting into the old kitchen where, yesterday, only the telephone had meant anything at all, squat and ugly on the dresser. Its message today was sweet enough: Paul could be collected at five.

Chris came back at four.

'I'll fetch him,' he said. 'I want to pick up the suit, too. Turner says the police up there have it. Carter wants it tomorrow. They're going to take it up. They're *interested*, Mother! It's all starting to come true at last.'

'What is, dear? Do drive carefully.'

'My life's work, Mother dear. Yes, I will drive carefully. I don't want anything to happen to my suit.'

'Is that the thing that saved Paul's life?'

'Yes. The very thing. Paul proved it, and now it's going to make my fortune.'

'Don't get Paul all excited. Remember he's coming out of hospital. Here are some clothes for him to put on.'

'Oh, Mother!' Chris was darting about the kitchen, kicking off his London shoes and groping under the dresser for his old sandals. He opened his brief-case on the table and pulled out a sheaf of newspapers.

'Look. Read all about it! You're on the front of one of them, looking like a startled rabbit. I must go, if they said five.'

He shrugged into an old jersey, snatched up Paul's clothes, and dashed outside to the Land-Rover. The cows were going back on to the marshes, and he skirted the slow ones gingerly, then sent the car bucketing down the drive. He sang as he drove, and the warm afternoon air streamed through the window. He picked up the suit from the police, then drove up to the hospital to collect Paul.

'Paul Fairfax? Just a moment,' the receptionist said; and Chris handed in the clothes and then strolled happily up and down the hall, reading the posters and the notices, too eager just to stand. In a few minutes Paul came down with a nurse.

'Chris! I was expecting Dad.'

'Hi, Paul.'

'I didn't even know you were home from Bavaria!'

'I arrived home in the middle of this old thing.' He paused, while Paul said good-bye to the nurse, then they walked out into the evening sun. 'The car's here. I collected the suit off the police.'

He opened the door for Paul. The suit was lying over the back of the seat. Paul looked at it, and a slight shudder passed over his face. Chris smiled at him, and pushed the suit into the back, out of the way.

'All right?'

'Yes. I'm all right.'

Chris thought Paul looked none the worse for his ordeal, but there was a reserve about him that he had not expected. A sort of quietness: a subtle thing that Chris could not quite recognize. He'd certainly had plenty of time to sort things out in his mind. Looking at him, Chris realized now, for the first time, just what he must have gone through.

'My word, Paul, you don't want to give us all a scare like that again——'

'I know. I'm terribly sorry. I didn't mean——'

'Sorry? That's not what I meant. What have you got to apologize for?'

'For being such a fool.'

'Don't talk such rubbish. You're no fool, you're a ruddy hero, coming through all that without going off your rocker. You knew the suit was defective, didn't you? That I only bunged a rough patch over the worst of that porous area?'

'Yes.'

'I thought you knew. Must have been a comfort to you, considering your situation!'

'I didn't think about it. But I wasn't brave, so don't say I was. I was a fool to miss the tide, a fool to hit the buoy, and scared out of my wits the whole of the time, right from the moment I left the Colne.'

'You know what, Paul?' Chris started the engine, and backed neatly out of the parking place. 'You're not a fraction of the fool you think you are. I've got a few surprises for you.'

'Such as?'

'That you've been right about a whole lot of things all along the line. That Winnington was a liar, for one.'

'Oh?' Paul glanced curiously at Chris. 'Has Gus told you the other things I said about him? Are they true, too?'

'I don't know what you told Gus. Did you tell him that Peter stole the idea of old Charlie here, and had it privately manufactured at Dunfort's?'

'I told him that he was stealing your idea, yes. And that he tampered with your light to make it go out that night, and with the suit to make it leak, and that I thought—although I'm not really sure about this—that they were intending to lose you that night when they sailed away from you.'

'Right, all along the line. Although we can't be sure, I agree, about the last bit.'

Paul looked at Chris, jerked out of his resignation. 'What do you mean? What has happened?'

Chris told him, right from when he left Proctor by the side of the lake in Bavaria.

'Then I *did* see *Woodwind*,' Paul said wonderingly. 'I thought I was having hallucinations.'

'And the whole thing, Paul, is part of a very much larger

thing. They didn't put Peter and Warner in clink—and no bail allowed either—for pinching my suit idea. That's just peanuts compared with the real goings-on. It seems the police already have a file on Peter. He's been suspected of selling industrial secrets, once to an Italian firm, and once in the States. When the police got aboard *Woodwind* they found that the two of them were clearing out with a whole load of secret guff that Peter had lifted from this electronics firm where he's been working for the last three years. They had been all ready to go, it seems, and my barging in just precipitated the move a bit. Helping himself to my idea, you see, was just a professional habit that Peter couldn't resist. He's a very clever man in his field—he knows a good idea when he sees it.' Chris chuckled.

'And Warner?'

'Warner was the brains behind getting a good price for whatever Peter managed to pick up. Peter's brilliance saw to it that he was able to get jobs where he was in on the very important stuff—always in the same line, of course, and Warner did the negotiations abroad. There's quite a bit of this going on, it seems, now all this sort of thing is so highly competitive in an international field.'

'I didn't guess at all that,' Paul said. 'I only thought——' He paused, and shook his head. 'I didn't like Peter, and I was so scared for you, trusting him over something so important. Do you think that night . . . Was he that bad?'

'That they'd wanted me to get drowned? It's hard to say. They knew the suit was leaking because Winnington had doctored it—I'm sure of that now—so if they *had* left me to it, I wouldn't have stood a chance. They could have kept the plans they'd already drawn out and gone ahead on their own. I'd already told Peter that it was my own idea. If anything had happened to me, I doubt if Proctor or any of the others in Cambridge would have gone on with it, and Peter would have had the whole thing to do as he liked with.'

'I think Peter didn't want to do it,' Paul said. 'That was why he was so quiet and nervous. He liked you, I think. I got the feeling that Warner tried to force him into it, and when I barged up screaming and yelling it was Peter's excuse to turn round and pick you up.'

'Did you barge up screaming and yelling?' Chris asked, amused.

'Yes. I knew something had happened. I don't know how. And I screamed at them. I'm always getting scared, and screaming about things,' he added softly.

'But, Paul, you've had good reason. You've been right all along. It was you who saw the truth of what was happening, not me with my head in the clouds.'

'Just a fluke, then,' Paul said.

'Think what you like. It's obvious you've done me a few good turns in your time. What about this last effort of yours, testing old Charlie here for thirty-three hours? Longer than I'd ever have managed if things had gone right for me? Did it ever occur to you that you were testing it in deadly earnest?'

'No. I felt it was more a matter of me being tested than the suit. And me sinking if the suit failed.'

'But you can see now? You did inadvertently what I've been trying to do since last Christmas. Everybody read about it in the newspapers, and all the people I had most wanted to get interested in the idea rang me up of their own accord. And my troubles are now over. The thing has been taken up by Dunfort's.'

'Because of my sinking *Swannie*?'

'Yes.'

Chris glanced at Paul as he lapsed into silence again. He looked very calm and contented, sitting there watching the combine harvesters that were working through the warm evening, and smiling, screwing his eyes into the brightness of the sun.

The following evening Paul went down to the sea-wall where *Swannie*'s old berth was. He sat on the sea-wall and waited for Gus, who he was sure would come, sooner or later. It was still hot. Both days, since it had happened, had been cloudless and golden, as if to show him what he had so nearly missed, and Paul could sit there and just look at it, and go on looking at it by the hour without losing his sense of awed satisfaction that he was still a part of it all. Everyone at home kept saying how quiet he was and looking at him anxiously, and Paul thought, if it had happened to them they'd be quiet, too, but he couldn't explain his feelings. He felt like one of those writing slates that he used to have in his Christmas stocking when he was little, which he had covered with writing and drawing and then magically erased by pulling it up out of its frame. When it was pushed back again it was all clean. He felt erased. How could he explain that?

Gus came at about seven, walking along the wall, his hands in his pockets. Paul went on sitting there, very conscious of Gus approaching, but quite unable to make any move to greet him. Gus wasn't hurrying either. Paul looked up.

'I thought you'd come,' he said.

'Hullo,' Gus said flatly. He sat down beside Paul on the grass and looked at him almost angrily. 'Oh, Paul,' he said. 'You——' He hesitated, and his glance dropped away to the spiky grass flattened under his legs. He picked a spike and put it in his mouth. 'You shouldn't do things like that.'

Paul smiled. They sat looking at the trough in the mud that *Swannie* had worn for herself during the years she had lain there, and the mooring warps that were neatly coiled on the bank, not saying anything. The tide was ebbing and a pair of oyster-catchers were dibbing for the morsels uncovered. Gus had watched the same pair two evenings ago in the same place, waiting for the sun to go down.

'You all right now?'

'Yes, of course. I'm sorry about *Swannie*.'

'What did you do? What happened?'

'I hit that wreck buoy. It was foggy, and I went below to make a cup of tea. It was a mistake, obviously.'

'Sydney said we might be able to salvage her,' Gus said. And then, 'It could have happened to anybody, a thing like that. The fog was pretty thick.' Gus rubbed his hair back wearily. His face was drawn and he looked worse from the ordeal than Paul. 'What a performance! Oh, Paul, it was terrible. I thought I'd killed you, making you go on your own. I never want to go through a thing like that again. And as for your part . . .' He shuddered, staring out across the water.

Paul looked at him, half surprised, half curious. He had expected banter or acrimony or scorn, but not remorse, from Gus, of all people.

'We weren't to know,' he said. 'You can't say it was your fault. I hit the buoy, didn't I? That wasn't your fault.'

'No. But I was pretty foul to you on Saturday, and it all sort of led on from there. I had an awful lot on my conscience, I can tell you.' He smiled, uncertainly. 'Has Chris told you all that's been going on? He must have done.'

'Yes.'

'And that you were right, what you said about Winnington?'

'Yes.'

'You see, I had that to digest as well. That you'd been right all along, and me saying you were off your rocker. Crikey, Paul, I'm glad they fished you out all right. Just for my own peace of mind, that's all.' He grinned.

Paul rolled over and lay on his stomach in the hot evening grass. There was a deep content inside him that he had never had since Mr. Glass had called in his white Jaguar.

'You know those plans have gone through?' he said to Gus.

Gus looked at him warily. 'They have?'

'Yes. They've been passed. The trimmings have been thrown out, the hotel and the swimming-pool, but the rest is on. They're starting it before Christmas.'

Gus didn't say anything. He looked at Paul, and chewed on his grass-stalk. Then, cautiously, he said, 'I'm sorry. For you, I mean.'

'Well, it's funny, but it all seems different now,' Paul said.

'What do you mean?'

'I still don't want it to happen. It's just that it doesn't seem to matter like it did. I've got used to the idea, I suppose.'

'What can you do, anyway? They push you around, and you've no choice. Getting mad just makes it worse.' Gus spoke his philosophy from habit, but Paul could see the light that had come into his eyes. There was no bitterness at all to go with the words, but the sort of excitement that he had when he had sailed *Swannie*. His unnatural repentance was forgotten. He was the old Gus, who had got what he wanted. Paul let him take it in, lying there as the sun disappeared and the shadow of the sea-wall merged into the shining darkness that was the un-covering shore. He wasn't sure, himself, why the plans for Birdsmarsh no longer had the power to hurt him as they had earlier. It wasn't that he no longer cared; it was as if what had happened had given him a new perspective on things. On himself, for a start.

'How crummy,' he thought. 'I'm a new man.' He smiled to himself in the dusk. 'Play it cool, boy,' he thought, and he knew that he could.